# SERAPHIM FALLS

SOME TOWNS HIDE THEIR SECRETS
BETTER THAN OTHERS.

D1726464

## T.R. TOTH

# Contents

# Keystroke

Emma was in trouble. She ran her fingers through her hair, digging at the scalp as they raked rows through the dark, tangled mess. Her elbows were starting to turn white because of the pressure she was putting on them to support her head.

She sighed heavily and slumped back in the black chair at her desk before leaning forward and grabbing a bottle of aspirin to help with her pounding headache. She reached for the remainder of the stale cup of coffee she had on her desk from earlier this morning.

Emma swigged back the brown, bitter liquid, and said a prayer this would work as well as help her get out of the mess she was in right now.

*He's going to kill me. I don't know what I'm going to do, but I have to come up with something.*

Trying as hard as she could, Emma still sat in front of the computer, blank screen staring back at her.

The sound of the bathroom faucet dripping in the next room and the ceiling fan overhead making its same unbalanced hum did little to help ease her headache.

*This is it, you can do this, Em.*

She gingerly placed her fingers on the keyboard and willed herself to start writing.

Nothing happened.

She collapsed her head on top of her folded arms on the desk. Was it dramatic? Yes. Did it make her feel better? A little.

When she was younger, her mother wanted her to go to those shady auditions that were looking for the next big "child star." But Emma saw them for what they were, cattle call for pedophiles, and refused to go.

Emma pushed herself away from the desk in exasperation and walked into the kitchen to refill her cup of coffee. In her experience, caffeine has done wonders to not only improve her headache, but her mood, too.

Her calico cat, Anastasia, wound her way between Emma's legs.

"I don't know why I can't come up with anything," she said while bending down and picking up the cat.

Emma placed her on the counter next to the coffeemaker and gave her a few scratches behind the ear before refilling her mug.

As the coffee enticed her with its smell, Emma tried to think of an idea for her newest book.

"I used to have so many great ideas, now I can't come up with anything."

After all, she was the famous Emma Greatwater, the author of the bestselling, "Bloodsuckers in Love," YA novels. Not only had the first two reached the top of the New York Time's Bestseller's List, but they had been made into feature films and started the careers of three of the hottest stars today.

Emma getting heat from her editor to write the next book before her readers cooled down for the dreamy, but cocky vampire teen and his moody, but beautiful, mortal girlfriend.

She scratched behind Anna's ear, left the room, and padded down the hallway back to her office.

It was brightly decorated with photographs of vacations Emma had gone on and artwork from her favorite artist Frida Kahlo.

Along a thin shelf, she had various photos from childhood, her college years, and more recent ones.

What usually stirred Emma's creativity, especially when she was in a dry spell, like now, was a photo she took of Earnest Hemingway's office in Key West. Living and writing in Key West was a dream of hers, and this photo of the tropical town was a reminder that maybe, someday, she could be just like Hemingway, going to the beach, petting lots of cats, and writing to her heart's content.

This time, while she was looking at the photo, Emma was drawn to the black object seated in the center of his desk surrounded by various hunting trophies and adventure photos.

Its sleek, black lines and shiny, metallic, push button keys immediately put a longing in Emma's heart.

"Maybe that's what I need to serve as my muse," she said. "Even if I would use the typewriter just to brainstorm, it might solve my writer's block."

Emma put her coffee cup on the desk and left to get her winter coat from the hall closet. She grabbed her hand-crocheted beret and bundled up to fight against the blustery, Pennsylvania, autumn afternoon. Emma fought against the wind to pull the door shut behind her as she left for her car.

As she turned her blue SUV into the parking lot of Grandma's Treasures, a local thrift store, she crossed her fingers hoping to find what she was desperately looking for. After all, Emma was pretty sure her local Walmart wouldn't have the typewriter she wanted, if they had any at all. With so many people depending on computers she was doubtful anyone would need one.

Emma got out of her car and walked to the store's front entrance. She pushed the door open, and a little bell softy jingled overhead.

The large front room was dimly lit by overhead lights and antique lamps scattered among side tables.

Treasures and junk were scattered from floor to ceiling thrown together in what seemed like a nonsensical order.

The air smelled like a perfume of musk, mothballs, and an old man's aftershave.

Emma daintily made her way through the room, stepping over piles of old sewing patterns, ancient books, and dishware with spiderweb cracks.

As she was passing a shelf crammed to the brim with clown figurines and carnival glass, Emma found something that took her breath away.

There it was.

In a darkened corner, left alone and forgotten, sat a worn, black typewriter. It was similar in style to the one Hemingway had on his desk.

Emma bent down, blew a thick layer of dust off the machine, and flipped over a tag that had "$25" written on it.

She carefully picked up her prize, which was heavier than she thought, and cradled it lovingly like a child comforting a stray puppy.

After navigating a path through the store, Emma plunked down the typewriter in front of the elderly man behind the counter who was engrossed with the morning newspaper crossword puzzle.

He was bald and the nearby lamplight shone off of him like a lighthouse bringing in stray shoppers as ships in the night carrying in cargo.

Emma inhaled deeply and found the source of the aftershave she had smelled when she first walked in. It was so strong; Emma swore she could taste it in the back of her throat.

The clerk took off his glasses, that he wore down on the tip of his nose and put them on top of the puzzle he had set down when he saw her coming.

"I forgot we had one of these," he said.

He had a kindly smile, the sort a grandfather reserves for his grandchildren.

"You do know how to use it, don't you?"

If anyone else would have said this to Emma she would have taken personal offense but seeing how sweet he seemed and the look of reminiscing on his face as he handled the well-worked keys, she let it slide.

"I think I can figure it out," she said.

The man nodded and reached under the counter to grab a liquor box to nestle the piece of mid-century technology in for safe traveling.

"If you don't mind me asking, in this day of computers, what are you going to do with this old typewriter?"

The man rung up Emma's purchase, took her money, and placed it inside of a cash register that looked like it belonged behind a soda fountain in the late 1800s.

"I'm hoping it'll provide some inspiration. I'm a writer and I have hit a dry spell. Maybe it will bring me luck."

The shopkeeper returned her change and slid the box across the glass countertop.

"Oh, I'm sure you won't have a problem coming up with new ideas now," he said. "Best of luck to you."

Emma thanked him and took the box to the car. She knew it was silly, but she couldn't help strapping it into the seat next to her. She wasn't sure how delicate the antiquated equipment was, and she didn't' want to have to scour eBay for replacement parts.

After pulling into her parking spot in front of her apartment building, Emma cursed herself for renting a place on the sixth floor without an elevator.

She lugged the typewriter up all six flights of steps without needing to stop for a break. Emma felt all her time doing cardio at the local gym was starting to pay off.

When she reached the door to her apartment, she put the box on the ground and dug out her keys. But, when she put the key in the lock, the door opened slightly without needing to be unlocked.

The blood drained from her face as she pushed it all the way open. Emma wracked her brain. In her haste to leave did she remember to lock the door? Could there be someone in the process of robbing her right now? Was she going to become the breaking news tomorrow morning on channel WKRV?

Emma shook her head. She was listening to too many true crime podcasts and was now overreacting.

She quietly stepped into the foyer and heard talking coming from her living room.

Emma gingerly sat the typewriter down inside the front door and picked up a baseball bat she named "Otis" that she kept near the entrance of her apartment as a way to defend against intruders. She never dreamed she would have to use him, but now here she was wrapping her fingers around the worn bat, gripping it like Babe Ruth ready to take someone's head off if need be.

She crept along the wall of the front hallway while her heart raced. Emma braced herself and counted to three before she peered around the corner into the living room. With Otis, poised over her head, ready to lower it onto the intruder Emma moved closer to the man who was sitting on her couch watching television.

*The audacity of this criminal to come in here and watch my TV. Why couldn't he just be a normal burglar and just steal my stuff and get out.*

Just as she was ready to slam Otis into this person's skull, the man turned, and a flash of recognition came across her face.

"What the hell, Noah?" Emma asked.

Noah turned around startled and saw his armed girlfriend standing behind him for the first time.

"Whoa! You know it isn't nice to sneak up on people. Especially with that in your hand."

Emma relaxed and returned the bat to her side.

"I didn't think I was sneaking up behind someone in my own apartment. Especially when said someone left the door unlocked making me think I was walking into a robbery in process."

Noah smiled, and ran his hands through his chocolate-colored hair. He loved how she inserted words that she heard from her podcasts into everyday conversations. He walked to her side, took the bat from her, and tossed it gently on a nearby chair.

He ran his hands down her arms and brought them up to circle his shoulders in a hug.

"I thought you would be here. But when you didn't answer I decided to let myself in and wait. Where were you anyway?" he asked.

Noah turned and leaned over the couch to grab the remote and shut off the TV so he could hear Emma better.

A smile grew across Emma's face as she held up one finger, meaning for him to wait a moment, and left to get her purchase.

"I went to get myself a little inspiration," she said while pulling the typewriter from the box. "I found this in hopes it would help stir some creativity."

Noah, who was a computer programmer and embraced all of the latest technology muttered "Luddite" under his breath before chuckling.

"What do you want with an old typewriter? Do you know how difficult these things are to use? What is wrong with your computer?"

"Nothing is wrong with my computer, Noah," she said.

Emma crossed her arms over her chest and looked away from her boyfriend.

"Something came over me to buy a typewriter. I just get this feeling that if I use this to do a little brainstorming, it might help me come up with new ideas."

Noah sighed as Emma left the room to go to the kitchen. She pulled out a bottle of wine she failed to finish last night and poured herself a glass.

Emma thought *It's five o'clock somewhere* as she justified her midday drinking.

She went back into the living room, wine glass in hand, and flopped down on the couch next to Noah.

Emma leaned against him and rested her head on the soft, blue flannel shirt he was wearing. She breathed in deep his cologne and the scent of sandalwood and oranges helped calm her mind.

"Frankly, I've hit a creative brick wall and my editor is barking at me every day to give him a new manuscript for the third book. But no matter how hard I try; I can't get the words on the page."

Noah turned and kissed her on the top of her head before putting her hand in his.

"I want you to realize you are a successful writer because of your ideas. Using a typewriter won't give you anything you already don't have. However, if it makes you happy and if you feel it will get the 'creative juices' flowing, then so be it."

Emma continued to sit there, feeling foolish, thinking a typewriter would solve all of her problems.

Noah let go of Emma's hand, jumped off the couch, and grabbed the box at Emma's feet.

He walked toward her office and put the new purchase in the center of the desk, just like Hemingway.

"It really does bring something to the room," he said." What do you say we celebrate your new purchase and go out to dinner?"

Emma planted a kiss on Noah's cheek. His suggestion seemed to lift her spirits.

"Sounds good," she said.

Noah turned to leave the office and walked down the hall.

"Let me use the bathroom first," he said.

While he was gone, Emma stood in her office and looked at the worn typewriter. It felt like it had always been there, and Emma had a hard time remembering what it looked like before its arrival.

As she turned to leave, Emma glanced at the photo of Hemingway's office and saw the majestic typewriter on the author's desk. She was lost in the photo when she felt a chill down her spine and saw a shadow reflecting off the glass of the photo. When she whirled around, the room was empty.

"I'm ready if you are?" said Noah. "Are you alright? You look like you're lost or something."

Emma looked at her boyfriend, and then shook away the uneasiness she was feeling.

*It must have just been a shadow or even my own reflection.*

"No. I'm fine. Just waiting for you, let's go."

Noah and Emma bundled up and headed out into the cold as the afternoon was turning into evening.

When Emma opened her eyes, the morning light blinded her. She rubbed her temples as she felt her head was going to crack open. She rolled over to look at the clock; its red numbers were flashing 10 a.m.

"I guess drinking a whole bottle of wine wasn't such a good idea," she said.

Anastasia, seeing Emma awake, slinked over and gently pawed her to make sure she was alive and well enough to feed her.

Emma sat up in the bed trying to fight the feeling of the room spinning.

She threw back the covers and shuffled her aching body into the bathroom where she filled a glass with water before reaching into the medicine cabinet for aspirin to help cure her hangover.

Figuring a hot shower would at least make the achiness go away, Emma turned on the water and stepped into the warm and welcoming steam.

When she finished, Emma fed Anna, made breakfast, got dressed, and finally went into her office. The excitement of trying out her new purchase from yesterday, was the only thing that made the morning bearable.

As she opened the office door, Emma was greeted with a surprise. A sheet of paper was already in the typewriter. When she went around the desk to sit down, Emma could see the page was already filled with text.

She put down her steaming cup of coffee and read the paper protruding from the top.

*The little girl, who wore her dark hair in twin braids cascading down the side of her head, bounded down the road while skipping rope. Her new pink sweatshirt that read "Cutie" in metallic letters gleamed in the sun. Suddenly, out of the corner of her eye, a beautiful butterfly fluttered in front of her and then continued down a side street. The girl followed the butterfly as it ducked through a chain linked fence and into darkness.*

Puzzled, Emma looked at the paper. She couldn't remember writing any of this. It didn't have anything to do with vampire teens and angsty love, so it didn't seem like her usual work. But, who else could it have been?

Realization dawned on Emma. She reached into her pocket for her phone, dialed a phone number, and waited.

"Hey, sweetie? Quick question: did you do any writing on my new typewriter?"

There was silence as Emma listened to Noah explain how he didn't have anything to do with it. They talked for a little, making plans for that evening, before she hung up and then returned to the typewriter.

She settled into her seat, took a swig of coffee, and decided to continue the story that was already started for her.

For the next three hours, Emma weaved a tale about the little girl, Carly, and how she followed the butterfly into a world of darkness that was full of nightmarish creatures who were twisted forms of people she knew and loved in the real world. The story was turning into a dark and evil "Wizard of Oz" except every character was more Wicked Witch from the West instead of Glenda.

Emma told of the girl's parents and sister, who in the real world, diligently looked for her and vowed to never give up.

When Emma reached the part in the story where Carly was trapped inside of the abandoned Lakewood Amusement Park, she heard a large crash somewhere in the apartment.

The sudden noise snapped her focus from the written world she had created back to her apartment.

As the hairs on her arms stood up, she pushed away from the typewriter and walked to her office door.

She didn't know what came over her and she felt she was in a trance-like state while writing her story.

Emma wasn't just writing about Carly. She could feel Carly. She was scared when Carly was alone and lost more hope each day she was away from her family. If Carly had tears running down her face, so did Emma.

Emma shook her head, trying to clear away the fog left behind from Lakewood Amusement Park and went to investigate the noise.

In the hallway, she looked out the window and saw it had turned to night.

*How long was I writing? This never happens.*

As Emma carefully walked into the living room, she began to grow afraid. It wasn't like her to lose track of time like this.

She looked at the table behind her couch and saw the answering machine was blinking a red number one. She had missed a call while writing? She never heard the phone ring.

Emma walked over to press the play button on the machine and heard a crunch under the slipper of her left foot. When she looked down, Emma saw the remains of a water glass lying on the floor in a pool of sparkling glitter.

She had no idea what caused the glass to be smashed on the floor like this. She was starting to panic. Emma could feel her chest starting to tighten like a corset being laced. She screwed her eyes shut and began to breath for four counts in, hold for four more counts, and release the breath for eight.

Eventually, Emma was able to calm down enough to take care of the mess. She went to the kitchen, grabbed a dustpan and broom, and swept away the debris. Emma was lucky she had slippers on or else she would be picking glass out of the bottom of her feet.

Emma eventually chalked it up to Anna trying to vie for attention by knocking down a glass she had left on an end table.

But, when she stood up to empty the dustpan, Emma saw the glass had broken too far away from any furniture. It would have had to been thrown, with great force to end up there.

Her mind was already reeling from writing so much she shrugged it off for the moment and walked back over to play the answering machine message.

"Hi, Honey. It's your mom. I was wondering if you would like to get lunch sometime this week and catch up. It's been a while. Give me a call. Love you."

Emma loved the sound of her mom's warm, sing-song voice. She made a mental note to call her back tomorrow. But now, her rumbling stomach was telling her to find something to eat. It seemed like the hunger hit her out of nowhere.

Emma opened the freezer door and was greeted with a blast of cold air that felt good on her flushed face. She reached toward the back and pulled out a frozen TV dinner.

"Sometimes, I think you eat better than I do, Anna," she said.

The cat looked up from lazily cleaning her paw in her cat bed in the corner of the room to give her a slight "meow."

Emma walked over to the microwave, popped in the meal, and set the timer.

While her dinner was cooking, she decided to make a copy of the progress she had made on her manuscript, and send it along to her editor, Alan Preachman.

*It's a little different than what I usually write, but at least it will give him something to read.*

She scanned the typewritten pages, attached them in an email, and shot everything to her editor.

Right after she hit "send" her microwave dinged. She left the office and walked back to the kitchen to pick up her dinner before sitting in front of the television to watch an episode of "American Pickers."

After finishing dinner, Emma could feel her eyes growing heavy and she struggled to stay awake.

Feeling like she accomplished a lot of work during the day, Emma decided to go to bed early.

She changed into her pajamas and pulled back the sheets so she could crawl under the downy soft covers. As she rolled over on her side to get comfortable her foot hit something near the bottom of the bed. One end of it was cold while the other long end was smooth.

Emma sighed, all she wanted to do was sleep, but knew she had to take care of this first. She reached down under the covers toward her feet and grabbed onto the mysterious object. It was long, smooth, and soft to the touch. When her hand emerged, she had her fingers wrapped around a belt. Well, at least it looked like part of a belt.

*I'm not sure how this got here, but it must have gotten tangled in the sheets when I was doing laundry.*

Emma dropped the slick, leather belt on the floor and decided worry about it tomorrow morning as sleep was starting to cloud her eyes.

That night, Emma didn't sleep very well. She tossed and turned while battling her way through a nightmare. In her restless dream world, Emma found herself stuck in a small room. There was only a little window with bars on one side and an opening covered with more bars on a heavy, metal door. The opening prevented Emma from any hope of escape. Besides a lumbering iron bed in one corner of the room, there was also a plain wooden desk with white paper and her typewriter. Emma felt terror creeping in on her. She opened her mouth to let out a blood curdling scream when the heavy door swung open. Before she had a chance to see who opened the door, Emma woke with a start. Her bedsheets were soaked, and her body was covered in a sheen of sweat.

Emma looked around and saw she was safe in her apartment and the morning sun was starting to creep into her windows. She was never so happy to see Monday morning than she was now.

She rubbed her eyes and tried to massage the sweat from her skin, but she couldn't stand the thought of its stickiness. Emma got out of bed and walked to her bathroom to take a shower. She let the warm jets pound her skin in hopes of washing away the horrible memory of being a prisoner in that room. She remembered the way it felt to be surrounded by the cold, cinder walls and the Spartan furnishings. Just thinking of it now made her chest start to tighten and panic creep into her throat.

Under the water, Emma shook her head and pushed away the nightmare with thoughts of her book and what plans she had for Carly next.

She stepped out of the shower and got dressed for the day before walking into her office to check her email. She hoped Alan had responded to the partial manuscript she had sent him.

When she switched on the light above her desk, Emma saw all of her typewritten pages were crumpled into violent looking balls and shoved into her trash can.

Emma became immediately scared. She knew she didn't destroy her work like this and was worried about how it happened. She reached into the wastebasket and tried to salvage the documents by un-crumpling and smoothing them on the desk with her hand.

Luckily, she was able to get the majority of wrinkles out. Then a light bulb went off. She had digital copies. She could feel some of the anxiety fade away.

After making a light breakfast, Emma positioned herself in front of the typewriter to continue Carly's story.

*No matter how hard she tried, Carly kept falling down the shaft that was under the carousel. She dug her fingernails into the wall in hopes of clawing her way out of the darkness but had no success. All she was left with was the bloody reminder of where her nails used to be on her nail bed. Her fingers were getting sore and bruised as she fell down into the depths again.*

Emma continued her story and switched to the perspective of the parents and sister as they organized the search party that was looking for Carly.

While the group was assembling, the sister seemed to be holding back information about Carly and any thoughts she might have about where she could be.

While she was typing, her computer made a noise to the side of her. Emma slid her desk chair over to it and jiggled the mouse to take it out of sleep mode. She typed her password to unlock the screen, where she opened her email to find a response from Alan, her editor.

*Emma received your manuscript. As your editor, and friend, I feel like I need to tell you this is a lot different from your usual novels and it is a tad dark and frightening. The lovesick teens who read your novels, and are your bread and butter, will be turned off by this divergence from your usual stuff. Are you sure this is what you want to submit as your next book? Call me; we need to talk about Carly.*

Emma shut the lid to her laptop with a huff. Alan had been hassling her about handing over any type of novel attempt and now he wants to be picky? But Emma didn't care what he said or even what her readers thought. She knew what she was writing would be a hit. Deep down inside, Emma knew she couldn't stop writing it. She was being compelled to write the story. A part of her even worried if she didn't finish it, then Carly would be lost forever.

Emma looked away from the computer toward the clock on the wall. The hands stretched and touched the numbers to make it 2 p.m. She had forgotten she called her mom earlier in the morning and would have to leave soon to meet her for a late lunch. They had planned to try the new Italian bistro two blocks away from her apartment.

Just as she was putting on her shoes there was a knock at the door. Emma shuffled toward it with one shoe on and the other in her hand. She tentatively peered out the peephole and saw her mom standing there. Emma reached for the deadbolt and unlocked the door.

"I'm not even late, yet. Give me some credit," said Emma while leaning over to put on her other shoe. "I was just on my way to meet you."

Her mother pushed past her and into the foyer with a worried expression on her face.

"I thought maybe we could chat a little before we went out," she said taking a seat on the blue couch in the living room.

Taken aback, Emma walked over and sat beside her moving one of the fuchsia, floral throw pillows out of the way before putting it over her lap while tucking her legs underneath her.

"You have such a beautiful view from here," she said trying to make polite conversation before she got into the meat of why she was at her daughter's apartment in the first place instead of meeting her at the restaurant like they planned.

"Emma, can I be honest?"

Emma laughed. It was a combination between amusement and frustration.

"When haven't you been," she replied under her breath, but all her mother heard was, "sure."

"I'm worried you aren't taking care of your personal life. You work on your novels all the time, and I'm concerned you are going to become so absorbed into them, you won't have time for your real life. I worry you are living in a fantasy world of your own creation."

Emma unfolded her legs and stood up from the couch to look at her mother. She was hurt and couldn't believe what she was saying. Sure, Emma had recently become absorbed in her work, but she had Noah in her life. A boyfriend should count for something.

Emma put her hands on her hips.

"Mom, I'm perfectly happy where I am. Noah and I are doing great. I'm fine. If there was a problem, I would let you know."

Emma's mother sighed. Making her daughter upset was the last thing she wanted to do. She reached out and held Emma's hand while looking at her with eyes full of sadness.

Before Emma could say anything about how she shouldn't be pitying her, her mom's phone rang. She reached for her purse and searched through it. When she found the phone, her mom walked back into the foyer before she answered.

From the bits and pieces of the conversation Emma could understand it was her father on the other end. She had no idea what they were talking about, but Emma could tell by her mom's nervous pacing it wasn't good.

Her mom hung up and came back into the room.

"Emma, honey, I know I just got here, but I have to go. Your father's car just broke down, and I need to pick him up from the garage."

Emma looked at her mom, disappointed they wouldn't' be going to lunch together. She felt that all her mother did was swoop in to insult her life and then run away, leaving her hurt and bruised. But she never shared how she really felt.

"Please tell me you will take care of yourself, and if you need help or someone to talk to, please call me."

"Mom I will. Stop worrying."

Emma's mother put her coat on and gave her daughter a tight squeeze before she left. After locking the door behind her, a disappointed and confused Emma walked back to her office to continue writing. Her worked seemed to be the only constant in her life recently.

For once in her life, Emma felt she was heading in the right direction. Noah was a great guy and they had been going strong for about a year now. She even thought a proposal would be in her near future. Emma thought that maybe if she was married her mom would finally see her as stable and wouldn't worry so much now that she had a family of her own.

Her books were also having a big impact on her life. No longer was she a struggling writer trying to get anyone to take her seriously. Now everyone was waiting for her next book to come out. She finally had a comfortable life because of a career she loved.

And now, she turned a corner with her new book.

Things were especially turning the corner since she found her muse, the typewriter.

Emma placed her fingers on the keys. Since she wasn't going to lunch, she figured she might as well start writing.

Her creative juices began to flow like gasoline through the engine of a sports car. Her fingers typed fast and full of fury over the keys as ideas came to her. Her hands had a difficult time keeping up with her head as she finished weaving the story of Carly, the little lost girl on the dark side of the world.

*"I'm here," said Carly as she pounded on the mirror in the bedroom she shared with her sister. "Please look at me."*

*Carly pounded with all the strength her weakened, little body could manage, but her sister kept reading her book, never once glancing in her direction.*

*A tear-stained Carly turned away from the mirror and walked hopelessly into the darkness to try and find another way back into her world.*

As Emma typed the last few words to the book, she felt a huge weight lifted from her chest and her body settled into complete exhaustion. It was as if she had been holding her breathe for a long time and now felt safe to let it all out. The relief was immense. She had no idea this novel took so much out of her. But, looking back at the huge stack of papers on her desk, Emma wasn't surprised at how tired she was. She had managed to write a complete 250-page novel in just seven days.

Sleep weighed heavily on Emma, so she picked herself out of the desk chair and shuffled into her bedroom. Unable to even change her clothes, Emma sank into the bed and drowsily pulled her legs under the covers as she drifted off to sleep, free from the compulsion to keep writing.

Feeling like she had slept for a full week straight, Emma strained to open her eyes. She rubbed them to break apart the crust of sleep. When she first started to open them, Emma couldn't see anything because the light streaming from the window was too bright.

But, when her eyes adjusted, she let out a scream of terror. Surrounding her were the same cinder block walls, barred windows, and heavy, steel door from her dream.

*I must still be asleep. This isn't real.*

Emma reached down to pinch her flesh between her fingernails and was surprised when she felt a shock of pain.

In her state, Emma tried to get out of bed, but found herself tangled in the blankets. Once freed, she ripped the sheets from the bed in her anger and saw two leather straps lying at the corners of the bottom of the bed.

Panic rose in her chest and the familiar tightening started to happen. No breathing exercise was going to be able to calm her down, and Emma knew she had to get help, quickly.

She ran for the door and started pummeling her fists and screaming to be let out. Her hands were starting to throb, and her throat was becoming raw.

While she was leaning against the cold, metal door she heard the clanging of a key being fit into the keyhole as the door unlocked.

She backed away and sunk to the floor as the familiar scent of sandalwood and orange filled her nose. Relief immediately flooded Emma's brain and her heart started to slow when she saw Noah walk in. She ran towards him and threw her arms around his neck.

"Noah, I'm so glad to see you. I was terrified and alone and now I feel so much better. Let's get out of here," she said.

Emma breathed deep, with each inhale bringing back pleasant memories of the two of them.

Noah pulled back from her and held her at arm's length while trying to pry her away from him.

"Miss, I'm going to need you to sit down and have a seat away from the door," he said.

Noah guided her back to a desk that was along one side of the room before he forced her to bend and sit in the chair.

"Noah what's wrong? Don't you recognize me? It's Emma, your girlfriend. We have to hurry up and get out of here."

Emma tried to fight and push against Noah. She couldn't understand why he was trying to force her into this chair. But no matter how hard she fought; Noah was too strong.

Emma's head and heart started to swirl. She wasn't sure what was going on.

*Why doesn't Noah know who I am? What happened?*

Emma had to wake up from this horrible nightmare.

Seeing she wasn't going to move on her own, Noah guided and then pushed Emma to the chair that was next to the black typewriter and stuffed calico cat.

Emma, confused, tried to push her way past the man she had thought was her boyfriend. The man she had dreams about a future with. Hell, she was even dreaming about what their future family would look like and how happy her mother would be to finally have a grandchild.

While Emma was thinking about all of her dreams that would never happen, Noah reached into the pocket of his white pants and pulled out a syringe. He gripped the plastic covering in his teeth, jammed the needle into Emma's upper arm, and pressed the plunger to dispense the clear liquid directly into her blood stream.

"Noah! What the hell are you doing? What's wrong with you? I love you!"

No matter how much she begged and pleaded with him, Noah's face remained distant and stoic. Like all the words and emotions, she was hurling toward him meant nothing.

As Emma sat in the chair, feeling the cold metal pierce her flesh, she looked at Noah's shirt and saw a name badge attached with a small clip that read: Noah Sanders, Orderly, St. Francis de Sales Hospital.

Emma felt the drug begin to take its affect and she started to relax. All of her muscles that were stretched tight like a rubber band on the verge of snapping, now felt like over cooked pasta from a chain Italian restaurant. It was like she was floating in the ocean, just bobbing along like a carefree seagull rising and falling with the tide. She no longer felt fear pumping through her veins, but a euphoria like state had replaced it.

"She's ready for you now, Dr. Preachman," said Noah.

He stepped out of the way for another man to enter before he left.

Passing through the doorway was a tall, older man with salt and pepper hair and a mustache that matched. He looked like the type of man that could turn off his kindness with a switch. One minute he would be taking his grandson fishing, and the next minute he was getting down to business at his job. But Emma felt his kindness won out most of the time. She didn't know this man until now, but she felt like she could trust him. After all, he was her editor.

*Finally, someone will listen to me.*

He grabbed a nearby chair, hiked up his pant legs, and sat down opposite Emma. He was poised with a clipboard in one hand, a pen in the other, and a serious expression across his face.

"Do you know who I am," he asked?

Emma wrinkled her face in disgust.

"Alan, I'm not in the mood for games. You are my editor, Alan Preachman."

The man made a few markings on his clipboard. He stopped writing and looked up at Emma. His expression had softened and was now replaced with a look of kindness mixed with sadness.

"Well, you are half right. My name is Alan Preachman, but I'm not your editor, Emma. I'm your doctor here at St. Francis."

Emma's mind began to swim. She wasn't sure if it was from the injected drugs or if she was really confused.

*Why is Alan playing this game with me? If he is trying to get payback for not having my manuscript in on time, I'm going to be very upset with him.*

Emma began digging her nails into the palms of her hands in an attempt to pull herself from the pool her brain was starting to sink into. She needed clarity.

"Emma, do you know why you are here," he asked.

Dr. Preachman reached over to her and grabbed her wrist to take her pulse and to prevent her nails from drawing blood from her already scarred palms. This was obviously something she did regularly when she was upset.

"No, Alan, why don't you tell me," she answered.

Dr. Preachman slumped back into his chair, tired from having to do this routine another time.

"Emma, do you remember when you were about twelve years old, your sister Carly disappeared one day while you were playing? You were with her and said she left to go follow a butterfly. And when she went through a chain linked fence, you said the darkness swallowed her up. You ran home and told your parents, and a search party was organized."

Emma slouched in the seat, trying to wrack her brain. This never happened in her real life she told herself.

"For three days the party searched for your sister and for three days you blamed yourself. You told me you felt like you could have done more. At the end of the third day your sister was found at the amusement park."

Emma sat forward so she could look closer into Alan's eyes. If she saw them better, maybe she would see he was lying.

"No, Alan. Carly isn't real. That's just the plot of my newest novel."

The doctor took a deep breath before continuing.

"You refused to accept her death, and you kept saying that wasn't her body because you could still feel her presence. You said it was a 'sister thing.'"

Dr. Preachman searched Emma for any flashes of recognition. When there wasn't, he continued with the story.

"Last year on the fifteenth anniversary of your sister's death, you thought you saw her in the mirror and tried to break it with your fists to get her out. Your mother, who was worried about you, came to visit you at your apartment. She found you covered in blood surrounded by pieces of the mirror. You were inconsolable, so your mother and father thought it would be best to check you in here, under my care."

Emma sat silently for a while trying to take in everything the man had just told her. She began to play with a thread that came lose on her pajamas. She wound it around her finger and pulled it tightly, cutting off circulation just to watch her pale skin turn red then purple.

*Was he trying to trick me? None of this seemed possible.*

Emma straightened herself in the chair, the best she could, and started at Alan dreamily.

"Why are you lying to me, Alan? You know I'm a successful young adult novelist. I told you before, you are my editor, and the story you are talking about is the one I sent you. It's going to be my newest novel. You even said, 'it was too dark for my audience of lovesick teens.'"

Alan looked at Emma with pain in his eyes.

"Emma, you THINK you are a famous novelist. In your mind, you have taken the identity of your favorite author, Carrie Austin. A few weeks ago, you asked for a typewriter because you were convinced it would be your 'muse.' We gave it to you because we thought it might provide a way to work through your repressed memories, especially since you were opening up about your sister for the first time in a long time."

"That's not true," said Emma.

She fought to stand up from the chair and to break through the surface of her drug induced haze.

Emma wobbled over to the nightstand next to her bed and grabbed the photo of Hemingway's office.

"I had this photo. I looked at it and thought a typewriter like this would inspire me, so I went to the thrift store and bought one."

Emma could feel herself becoming frantic again. She tried to slow and control her breathing, it helped a little, but she still felt like a runaway train ready to jump its tracks.

She ran her hands through her hair and wrapped her fingers around the dark strands. She began to pull and tear at her scalp to relieve some of the pressure, but the only thing she accomplished was having clumps of her hair, the ends tainted with blood, coming out in her hands.

Sandalwood and orange floated into the room again as Noah came back and helped Emma to her chair. This time he remained standing behind her.

"There was a man there, he sold it to me. You can go and talk to him at the store called Grandma's Treasures," said Emma.

Her words were rolling around in her mouth and her head. She wasn't even sure if she believed herself anymore. It seemed like someone else was reaching around in her brain, taking her thoughts, and twisting them so they would come out differently.

Dr. Preachman sighed heavily from his seat. He stood up, opened the door and stepped out for a moment, not closing it all the way, keeping his foot in the jam.

The scent of heavy aftershave, the kind an older man would wear, sailed into the room in front of a gentleman with a kind smile. It was the man who sold her the typewriter from the store.

Emma's heart started to flutter. She felt vindicated and finally things would start to make sense, her editor would believe her and this whole thing would just be a confusing mix up that her and Noah would laugh about later.

"Is this who you are talking about," asked the doctor?

"Yes! That's him," said Emma.

She grabbed the edge of the metal chair with one hand while pointing at the man with the other.

"This is Gary, he works here. He is the one who brought the typewriter to your room after you asked for it. Emma, you haven't left this facility in over a month."

With that Dr. Preachman nodded a silent thank you at the man who turned and left the room.

Emma couldn't believe what she was hearing. She knew she had been out of this room. In fact, this was the first she has seen of this room except for the few nightmares she had.

*What is happening to me?*

Dr. Preachman returned to his seat and began to talk to Emma again.

"After one of the orderlies accidentally broke a glass on the floor, and it shattered into pieces, you became upset because it brought back memories of the mirror that you broke at your house. Your writing became more agitated and so did you. We discussed it and thought it was best to destroy your manuscript and throw it away in your trashcan. But, before the can could be emptied, you found it. You were so angry that you started to work on it again, even more fiercely than before.

"During your computer time, you 'sent the manuscript to me' as your 'editor.'

"And that is why we need to talk about Carly. So here we are."

Alan made another note before he continued. The only sound in the room was the scratching of the pen on paper.

"We even called your mother to pay you a visit. She tried to stay for a while, but it was too hard on her, so she left shortly after she got here."

Emma's head began to spin. She was not sure what reality was anymore. She felt alone and frightened like a lost child.

As fear consumed her, she let out a harrowed scream while she pushed herself out of the chair and shoved Alan away when he got up to try and control her.

Before she could wrap her fingers around the frigid metal handle of the door, she felt a sharp biting pain in her neck.

Suddenly, the world faded away, and she fell into a deep sleep as her body slumped to the ground.

Emma stared out into the darkness and screamed for someone to help her.

As her eyes adjusted to the lack of light, she saw a little girl with dark braids and a pink sweatshirt with "cutie" written in metallic letters come skipping over to her.

"Hello, Emma. I've been waiting for you."

# Mr. Winston's Deal
# of a Lifetime

The room was crowded with people from Seraphim Falls and the air smelled of flowers.

Mr. Carl Winston stood next to the casket surrounded by roses, lilies, and daisies, the former Marjorie Huffman's favorite flower.

The line of people waiting to pay their respects to the former president of the Methodist Church Lady's Auxiliary, treasurer of the Friends of the Seraphim Falls Public Library, and volunteer at the local food pantry, snaked all throughout the viewing room.

Carl had a hard time imagining how many people cared about Marjorie and was happy to see the big turnout.

He looked over at his girlfriend and gently smoothed out a wrinkle that had formed on her light pink blouse.

*Marjorie always liked to look perfect. She would hate to think that I would stand here and let this happen.*

Sadness welled in Carl's eyes and threatened to boil over, until he felt a tap on his shoulder, bringing him back to reality.

"How are you doing, Grandpa?" asked a man in his late twenties who leaned in and gave him a hug.

"I didn't expect to see the famous Noah Sanders here. Shouldn't you be on a book tour somewhere?" asked the older man who was happy to see his grandson, who had recently penned a horror novel on the New York Times Best-Sellers List.

Noah laughed and shook his head, slightly embarrassed by the fuss that was being made over him.

"It's not every day the best-selling author of *Carly's Nightmare* is back in Seraphim Falls," said Carl beaming.

"Grandpa, stop. I wanted to come home to see you. I know how special Marjorie was to you. How are you holding up?"

Carl looked back at the woman who was laying there before him. It looked like she was peacefully sleeping, but he knew better.

"I'm okay. I'm going to miss her, but I've made peace with it. We had some great time together, but now I need to say goodbye."

Noah looked at his grandfather and gave him an understanding smile before a woman from the church came up and took over the conversation causing Noah to say goodbye.

For the next four hours, Carl stood faithfully by his departed girlfriend who he had dated for four years. Four years of eating dinner, challenging each other to *Jeopardy,* and people watching in the park across the street from her house.

Now Carl would need to find a new way of living, alone.

It would all have to start tomorrow morning when he would meet with Marjorie's attorney to go over her will.

Carl went and put the key in the lock. He had a difficult time turning the key and opening a door. Even though his Marjorie was gone, it still felt like he was trespassing.

Her modest, yellow, one story house, with a wrap-around porch with dormers and a maliciously manicured garden, always felt like home to him. But today, everything seemed strange and unfamiliar.

Deep down, Carl knew no matter how long he stood there it wouldn't bring her back and it wouldn't change the fact he had just inherited her house.

Carl turned the key and gently pushed the door open. A slight puff of dust was released when the door pushed inward. It danced through the morning sunbeams shining through the large picture window in the front living room.

Greeting him was the home she had made throughout her lifetime. It seemed like everything was still in its place waiting for her to come back.

Carl passed through the living room that was painted a pale blue and set up with a comfortable sofa, coffee table and two chairs angled toward a fireplace that was the focal point of the room. Right above the fireplace was one of Marjorie's pride and joys, a reproduction of Monet's "Water Lilies and Japanese Bridge." He smiled as he remembered when they visited the artist's traveling exhibit at the local museum and how excited Marjorie had been to see it.

Carl continued on and pushed through a swinging door and went into the kitchen to put the keys on the island.

Sitting in the center of the gray marble countertop were a bunch of white daisies, the last flowers he bought for her while she was still alive. Now they, just like her, were dead.

He walked over and threw the flowers away in the trashcan under the sink and washed the vase before putting it into a cabinet holding her glassware.

He cut through the other door of the kitchen and walked into the dining room. A small, light oak table sat in the middle with six chairs surrounding it. Carl remembered how much laughter and food was shared around the table. Marjorie was one for always having a party and gladly would welcome anyone to her table.

Carl continued his tour and walked to the first of three bedrooms. This was Marjorie's room. Her bed was covered in a quilt that she had received as a gift from the ladies' sewing circle for her dedication to the local library. There were a few dressers, a jewelry armoire full of costume jewelry, and her closet housing her nicer clothes were what was in the modestly sized master bedroom.

Carl began to feel overwhelmed at the fact that it was up to him to take care of all of Marjorie's things. He wondered how could one person be the sole caretaker to everything a person has gathered throughout their lifetime?

The clothes in her bedroom, all the cat figurines she had collected over the years, photo albums stacked on the bookshelf in the living room, all now belonged to him. She never married and had no children. The only nieces and nephews she did have lived across the country and couldn't be bothered to take care of the affairs of an aunt whose only communication was a card each Christmas.

He walked back into the kitchen, grabbed a glass from the cabinet, and filled it with water from the tap.

Carl had hoped the water would help him calm down and overcome the overwhelming feelings he was having.

He took the glass to the island and sat a stool to steady his thoughts.

He knew what he had to do.

Carl pulled a phone from his pocket and dialed the number to a local charity shop called "Grandma's Treasures."

"Hello, can I please speak to your manager?" he said to the person on the other end of the phone as he absentmindedly traced the veins in the marble counter tops.

"Yes, hello. I just recently inherited a home with all of its contents, and I wanted to see if your store would be interested in picking up donations?" he asked.

A brief pause stretched as the person on the other end of the phone talked.

"I will take whatever I want with me today, and you can come by at 9 a.m. tomorrow and take whatever you like. What's left will be picked up by a junk service."

Carl hung up the phone and stood up. He had in his mind some things he had wanted to take with him including a few photo albums, a sweater that smelled like her, a couple of knick-knacks including a spotted cat figurine that he bought her last Christmas, and a first edition copy of a book they both loved.

Carl walked toward the front door; all of his memories packaged in a single cardboard box that was previously used for shipping liquor. Then he looked around.

"See you on the other side, Marjorie," he said taking one last look around the room. He knew, after tomorrow morning, everything would be different.

"I think you are going to be very happy about this, Mr. Winston," said a taller man, in his early twenties with dark, slicked-back hair and wire-rimmed glasses. "Since Poplar Lane is a desirable street, in a desirable neighborhood, I think I can get premium dollar for the house."

Michael Constance, the top realtor in Seraphim Falls, according to his billboards, walked around the three-bedroom, two-and-a-half-bathroom house with a finished basement.

"The proximity to the park alone, Mr. Winston, will be a big selling point for families. The parents will be able to relax while they watch their children play across the street or in the spacious front yard," said Michael walking over to him. "I'm thinking of listing this in the high \$200,000. That way we will have a little wiggle room to come down if we need to."

Carl was taken aback. In his wildest dreams, he never thought this house would fetch that much money.

"I'll let you think it over. You can call me back later today and let me know if you want to move forward. If you say yes, I can have it listed this afternoon."

Carl shook the man's hand after taking his business card and drove home, his mind reeling about what he should do.

As he was eating lunch, in his own modest house, at a small kitchen table set for one, he thought about what Michael had told him. With the money from the house, he could afford to do some repairs on his own house, and maybe call up Eddie Carmichael, his friend for the past twenty years, and see if he wanted to go on their dream Alaskan fishing trip.

Besides, it would do no good to let the house sit there and rot alone. Marjorie would have wanted him to be happy and get as much as he could for her house.

Carl put down his sandwich and walked over to the phone that sat on the counter of his kitchen. He pulled out the business card from his pocket and punched in the number.

"Mr. Constance, we have a deal," he said to the other side of the receiver.

It had been a month since the closing on Marjorie's house. Because of a bidding war for the house, it was sold over the asking price for $310,000. After paying his attorney fees and closing costs, Carl walked away with $299,000, free and clear.

Carl began paying to have work done on his home, and he and Eddie had already booked their fishing trip to Alaska for next summer. They were both counting down the days until they would be on the other side of the country, up to their waders in the clear water of a new frontier.

Carl was even thinking of trading in his old jalopy for a newer car. He had always dreamed of owning a luxury vehicle, and he felt that now was the time. He could picture himself behind the wheel of a new, sleek, black Lincoln with heated seats and a cool-touch steering wheel.

He thought about this a lot as he drove to Smithon's Market, Seraphim Falls' only grocery store.

Carl grabbed a cart, pulled out his list, and went up and down the aisles, getting enough food to last him for a week. He hated grocery shopping but found produce never lasted more than seven days, so each week he went through the ritual of pacing through the store, humming to the pipped in elevator music, while trying not to be depressed that he was buying frozen dinners for one.

He grabbed cans of soup, tuna packets, and some of his favorite chocolate and peppermint candies. He always enjoyed sneaking one of these right before he went to bed.

Just as Carl was reaching for a jar of spaghetti sauce, he literally bumped into a woman who was reaching for the same thing.

"I'm so sorry, ma'am. You go first," said Carl taking a step back so the woman could get to the jar first.

"No. It's my fault, you go ahead," she said looking at him, her blue eyes shining with a giggle.

The woman looked to be roughly around his same age of sixty-five. She had chin length wavy white hair that still had some golden streaks running through it. She had a medium build and height and was dressed in a light summer sweater and blue jeans. She wore a wooden necklace that was made of different painted beads.

Everything about her screamed she was a creative and free spirited. Not a "wild-child" sort of person, but a woman who lived life on her own terms.

Carl returned the smile, his dark green eyes crinkling behind his glasses, and reached for the jar of sauce and handed it to her.

"I insist," he said. "My momma raised me to be a gentleman."

She took the jar from his hand and tucked her pale, wavy hair behind her ear.

"My name is Pauline O'Claira," she said extending a hand to him.

"Carl Winston," he said taking her hand in his and shaking it. "You must be new here. I don't think I've seen you around and this is a small town."

"Just moved here. I wanted a new start on things. My husband, who recently passed, and I used to vacation here, so I thought it was a beautiful place to move to," she said with a little sadness replacing the smile.

"I'm so sorry for your loss," said Carl. "I lost someone very special to me recently."

They both stood in silence for a moment, looking around the store, not sure what to say next. Pauline shifted the jar in her hands as Carl trade his weight from one foot to the other.

"You know what?" said Pauline breaking the silence with the cheerfulness returning to her voice. "Since we both have the same great taste in sauce, and I'm sure you agree eating alone is just sad, why don't I have you over for spaghetti tonight."

Carl began to panic a little. He was hoping he wasn't seeming like he wanted her to invite him over. That would have been too forward of him considering they just met.

"I couldn't do that. I would be imposing," said Carl, a little flustered at the idea.

"Nonsense. I invited you, so it wouldn't be imposing," she said while grabbing a piece of paper out of her purse and scribbling down the address. "Be here at 5 p.m. sharp. If you are late, you do the dishes."

She smiled at him and walked away to continue her shopping, leaving Carl to stand there, scratching the top of his head that was mostly bald except for white tufts on the side.

It seemed like his evening just got more interesting.

At ten minutes to five, Carl showed up at Pauline's home on Mountain Laurel Drive. He was surprised at how big the house was for one person. It was white with a purple and blue trim that had gingerbread designs tucked into its various nooks and crannies.

On the left-front portion of the house boasted large bay windows on the first and second floors. The roof above this area featured a steeple that was home to a carousel horse weathervane.

The wrap-around porch was the highlight of the home with the porch swing being a cherry on the Victorian sundae.

It reminded him of a bed and breakfast he and his late wife had stayed in once about 30 years ago. This was before cancer took her from him when she was only 32.

He nervously adjusted his tie, held tight to the lilies in his hand, and rang the doorbell.

Only a minute had passed before Pauline appeared in the glass storm door wearing an apron covered in lemons over a chambray shirt and long, flowing, black skirt.

"I'm so happy you came, Mr. Winston," she said beaming at him. "And you're even early. Please come in."

"These are for you. I hope you like them. I'm not sure what kind of flowers are your favorite, but I think everyone likes lilies," he said nervously prattling on while handing the flowers toward her.

Pauline reassured him by placing a gentle hand on his arm while taking the flowers from him.

"They are my favorite and they are very beautiful," she said while inhaling deeply and ushering him inside.

Once he stepped into the foyer, Carl realized how big Pauline's home actually was compared to his own.

A dark, wooden staircase wound all the way to the upstairs, and a stained-glass window of a red rose was in the gable above the door.

To the right was what must have been a formal parlor with built-in bookshelves and a wood burning fireplace surrounded by white, pearled tile.

Pauline held her hand out and indicated she wanted Carl to go to the left into what looked like a dining room. He followed behind her and, on the way, he remarked about how lovely her home was and admired all the polished, original wood and carvings of the house.

"I know it's big, but it felt like home when I first saw it, so I thought, what the hell!" she laughed while pointing at a chair for him to sit down. "I'm going to put these in water and then I will be back with our wine and pasta. Please feel free to help yourself to the salad."

Pauline left Carl alone. He looked around the room at the crystal chandelier and the China cabinet full of what looked like precious bone china. Everything seemed to be in its proper place, which seemed a little out of place for the free spirit that was Pauline.

Carl grabbed the crystal salad bowl, that looked like it originally was used for punch, and filled his plate and then Pauline's with salad.

After a few minutes, Pauline returned with two glasses and a bottle of Cabernet Sauvignon. She uncorked it and poured before she left again to return with plates of spaghetti and meatballs covered in the marinara sauce that brought the two of them together over dinner.

"I have a confession," she said while idly twirling the pasta on her fork. "I added a secret ingredient into the sauce."

Carl looked over at her and put his fork back on the plate.

"Oh?" he said not knowing if he should be worried or not.

"It's just wine, silly," she said while playfully tapping him on the arm. "I find it gives it a little kick."

Carl smiled and tasted the pasta and he agreed. The wine did make an improvement.

"So, Pauline, what do you like to do for fun?" he asked before taking a drink of the wine.

Pauline finished chewing and wiped her mouth. "Well, I have to admit that I love true crime stories. I like reading books about them, watching movies or television programs, and even podcasts."

"Podcasts? What are those?" asked Carl who wasn't interested in the latest technology. His old-fashioned flip phone suited him just fine.

"They are like radio shows, but you can listen to them anytime you want. It's really fascinating," she said. "Also, I like getting together with my friends at the sewing circle and when fall comes around, I love to hunt."

"Hunt for what? Bargains?" asked Carl half making a joke and half being serious.

Pauline's eyes twinkled and she laughed her full body laugh where she would throw her head back and open her mouth wide.

"Of course not! Hunting, like deer, rabbit, bear. My husband was a game hunter and I learned from him. He even taught me how to butcher properly," she said stabbing her fork into another bite of pasta.

Carl looked at her. The thought of woman hunting took him back. And the fact that she also knew how to butcher made him uneasy. He hadn't noticed that he started pushing his remaining food on his plate while he thought about the woman across the table from him with a loaded rifle in her hands.

Pauline could tell Carl was feeling uncomfortable by the way he was swirling the wine in his glass.

"What do you say we clean up these dishes and have coffee and dessert on the front porch?" she asked.

"I think that would be a lovely idea, but only if you let me help clean up," said Carl standing from his chair.

Pauline started to protest, but when Carl wouldn't hear of it, she gave in.

Together they stacked all the plates, grabbed the dinnerware and wine glasses and went through a door behind the dining room table.

In the kitchen, she washed, and he dried. They seem to fall into an easy routine that made it seem like they had been doing this, together, forever.

Maybe it was their past marriages and relationships that made it seem old hat, but it felt like there was a deeper connection.

That evening, Carl Winston and Pauline O'Claira shared peach pie and coffee as they laughed, talked about their future, and watch the sunset and the streetlights come on. It was the first of many perfect evenings they would spend together.

Throughout the rest of the summer, the pair had become inseparable.

The went strawberry picking, escaped the heat in movie theaters, took turns cooking dinner for each other, and even sneaked a few secret kisses on a walk to the town's famous falls.

Neighbors began to see them as a couple, and it made Carl and Pauline very happy to no longer feel like they were alone.

As summer started to fade, and the leaves put on a show by displaying their best colors, Pauline began to plan for a hunting trip that would take her out of town for a few days.

"Are you sure you don't want to go with me?" she said while sitting on the porch swing, her head on his shoulder, the evening before she was supposed to leave.

"No thank you. That's not my thing. You just be safe and enjoy yourself. I want you to come back to me in one piece," said Carl giving her a kiss on top of her wavy, white hair that was cut into a trendy looking bob.

"No worries there. I'm a professional," she said. "I do need to ask you a favor."

"Anything, you know that" he said.

Pauline sat up more on the swing and dug into her pocket. She pulled out a key on a maple leaf keychain and passed it to Carl.

"Can you come and check on my house while I'm gone for the weekend. You know how cantankerous these old houses can be. I wouldn't want to come home and find my living room flooded," she said.

Carl took the key and tucked it in his shirt pocket.

"No worries there. Leave it to me."

The next day, around four o'clock, Carl decided he would go to Pauline's house to make sure everything was okay. She trusted him, and he didn't want to let her down.

Carl pulled into the driveway, unlocked the door and went inside. It seemed so empty to him now that Pauline wasn't there. The house seemed even bigger than it already was, which was an amazing feat given its already huge size.

He checked everything on the first floor including the sink in the kitchen, windows in the living room, and toilet in the powder room.

As he walked upstairs to check on the five bedrooms and three bathrooms, the stairs creaked under him. With each groan from the ancient wood, Carl began to feel uneasy. It was like he was living in a haunted house.

Once he reached the top, he felt like someone was behind him. But when he turned, he saw nothing.

The first four bedrooms and all the bathrooms checked out. But, when he got to a spare bedroom he had never been in before, he had a hard time opening the door. He turned the knob, and it turned but it seemed the doorframe wouldn't release the door. He pushed on it with his shoulder, but it still wouldn't budge. Finally, after leaning back even further and then slamming his arm into the door, it pushed open and allowed Carl inside.

Immediately he saw what the problem was. Pauline had accidentally left the window open. It must have caused either the door to swell or a vacuum to form.

He walked over to shut the window when he realized he had stepped on something. A decorative basket with a lid laid on the floor with all of its contents spilled on the pink Oriental rug.

"Damn it," said Carl as he bent down and put everything in the basket. He was caught by surprise when he found a bottle of arsenic, unbroken, on the floor.

He turned it over in his hands.

*What could she be doing with this stuff? This isn't something to mess around with. I'll have to ask her about it when she gets home.*

Not knowing exactly what to do, Carl, put all the things back into the basket and found its place on the end table in front of the window he had just closed.

He left the room shutting the door tight, behind him.

After her weekend away hunting, Pauline returned victorious with a black bear that she had nabbed in the nearby woods of Marianna County. She even turned the fur into a bearskin rug for in front of the fireplace in her parlor and turned the meat into several meals of pot roasts, meatloaves, burgers, and stew.

But, when Pauline returned, Carl couldn't help but feel there was something different about her. Her usual sweet demeanor and laughing eyes became darker and she wasn't as warm toward him. He could almost feel her recoiling whenever he would bring his arm around her.

One day, while they were doing their usual evening ritual on Pauline's front porch of watching the sunset, the distance between the two of them had become so bad, Carl had to speak up.

"Pauline, I need to ask you something," he said while taking his arm off her shoulder and squaring himself to look at her.

She sat up and turned to him.

"What's going on? You seem so different anymore," he continued.

Pauline looked at Carl not understanding what he was talking about.

"Ever since you came back from your hunting trip, you seem changed. You don't laugh as much, you don't seem like you want me to touch you, and you're shorter tempered. Did I do something wrong?"

Pauline returned his look. She played with a glass bead bracelet that was on her wrist as she processed things over in her mind before reaching for his hand and taking it in hers.

"You know, Carl. I did some thinking while I was away. I'm sorry I have been so preoccupied. Going back to that cabin made me become so confused about what I really wanted out of life," she said changing her gaze to look toward the sunset. "When I was in the woods, I thought that I wanted to return to my old life. To move back. But the more time I spend with you, the more I feel like right here is where I want to be. I've just been so preoccupied worrying about this in my head, that is why I'm a little distant and snippy. I'm sorry."

Carl felt bad for her. He didn't want to upset her, he just wanted to know where their relationship stood. He remembers those days of feeling lost, even just recently with the passing of Marjorie.

"I'll tell you what," she said, gently slapping his knee while seeming to be back to her old, chipper self. "Why don't you go into the sideboard in the dining room and grab a new candle to replace this one that is burning out. When you come back, let's talk about a weekend getaway, a fresh start for us."

Carl loved this idea and happily went inside to get a new candle. He walked into the dining room and found the heavy oak sideboard, with maple leaves carved into it, and pulled out the top drawer.

He moved lace tablecloths and silver polish out of the way but couldn't find the candle.

When he opened the second drawer it slid out while making a soft jingling sound. He moved the table pad for the dining room so he could get a better look inside. But all he found on the bottom of the drawer were several gold bands.

Carl wasn't sure what they were at first. He picked up one and turned it over between his fingers. The light was reflecting off the worn band. He looked inside and could see something written there. He used his shirt to wipe away the dirt that had accumulated and saw an inscription that reads "K +P."

*This looks like a wedding band.*

He picked up another one. "J+P"

Carl looked at all of them and saw they definitely were wedding bands that each had a different inscription inside.

*What would Pauline be doing with all of these bands in this drawer? Why does she have all these?*

Carl began to panic. He wasn't sure why, but he felt like he had stumbled onto something that he shouldn't have seen.

He hurried up and put all the bands back in the drawer with the table pads on top. He shut it quietly and opened the one below where he found the candle that he was looking for.

Carl returned to the foyer and opened the screen door.

"There you are. I was starting to think you had gotten lost," said Pauline, her famous wrinkled eye smile back in place. "Find everything you were looking for?"

Carl paused for a moment.

*Did she know that I found something I shouldn't have? Why is she looking at me like that?*

"Yep! I got the candles," he said turning his back to Pauline and lighting the one he retrieved from the dining room.

He then walked over to the swing and took a seat next to Pauline, putting his arm around her. Her head rested on his shoulder.

For the next month and a half, the couple became inseparable again. Pauline and Carl decided to take their dream vacation, a nine-day cruise to Bermuda, and he finally bought the luxury car he had always dreamed of. Pauline inspired him to live life to the fullest.

They were eating more at fancy restaurants and trying new wines from regions they hoped to visit someday when they took a vacation to France. Pauline also enjoyed the lavish jewelry Carl gifted her for Christmas.

Carl felt he had finally met his match and was even toying with the idea of proposing to her when he got back from his fishing trip with Eddie this summer.

Everything was going so well until Carl received a call one cold, January morning.

He had just finished his breakfast and was washing his dishes in the sink when the phone on the counter rang.

Carl groaned, his arms up to suds in the sink. He shook them off, wiped them on his pants and snatched the phone from its receiver.

"Hello," he said, a little on the exasperate side.

"Is this Mr. Carl Winston?"

"It is. Who is calling?"

"Sir, my name is Andrew Harmon and I'm from ABN Bank. I wanted to talk to you about a problem we have encountered concerning your account."

Carl didn't answer right away. The blood was draining away from his face and pooling into a pit in his stomach causing his breakfast to churn like it was in a washing machine.

"What is it?"

"It seems, sir, that you have overdraft your account by $5,000. We thought this might be an error in our part, so we ran everything again. But unfortunately, the result is the same. We are going to need you to transfer money into your account to cover this cost."

"I don't have any other accounts," said Carl growing more anxious.

"Sir, maybe you have some investments or stocks that you could cash in to cover this, then."

Carl thought for a moment. Everything he had, including the money from Marjorie's house was in that one account. He couldn't believe that he had run through all that money.

Not wanting to sound like an idiot, "Yes. That's what I can do. How long do I have to get you the money?"

"A week, sir."

"Okay. You will have it in a week. Thank you," he said, hanging up the phone, not waiting for an answer.

Carl pulled out a chair from the kitchen table and sat down. He put his head in his hands. He began to feel like the room was spinning around him. Where was he going to get this money?

He thought about selling back his new car, but it was sold as-is and there was no way he would get back what he paid for it. He would be at a major loss.

Carl paced around his kitchen. The only thing he could come up with would be to cancel his and Pauline's upcoming first-class, round trip train tour to wine country. The deposit should cover his overdraft.

He didn't want to disappoint her, but he had no choice.

Carl sighed and picked up the phone to call Pauline and tell her the bad news.

"Hello," said her cheerful voice on the other end.

"Hey, honey. I'm afraid I have some bad news."

"Are you okay? You're not sick or anything?"

"No, it's not that. I'm afraid we are going to have to cancel our wine trip."

There was silence on the other end before she spoke.

"Why is that?" she asked, her voice becoming less cheerful and more irritated.

Carl was so embarrassed, he didn't want to tell her the truth, but felt like he had no other option.

"I'm broke. I'm out of money. I spent it on our vacations, my car, making repairs to my house, expensive jewelry. I over drafted $5,000 and now I need to cover that. The only way I can do that is to get the deposit back for our trip."

Silence was once again on the line.

"Are you still there?"

"Yes," she said hesitantly. "Look, I have a pie in the oven and the timer is going off, so I'm going to have to go."

"Is that a pie for our dinner tonight? I can't wait to try it," he said, some happiness returning to him.

"I'm sorry. I thought I told you. I have my sewing circle tonight. The pie is for them."

Carl deflated.

"What time will you be home? I can come over after."

"Tonight, isn't going to be good. How about I call you tomorrow. I really have to go. Goodbye, Carl."

The phone went dead.

Carl sank even lower in his chair. It seemed like he was losing his love all over again. It was feeling just like when his wife and then Marjorie died.

That night, he warmed a frozen TV dinner in the microwave. As he watched the cardboard tasting turkey dinner rotating in the appliance, he grew more depressed. He then ate it on a tray in the living room while watching Jeopardy by himself. It seemed so lonely without Pauline there to shout out the answers with him.

When he went to bed, he tossed and turned. It wasn't just about the money, but it was about how Pauline had rushed him off the phone when she found out he wouldn't be able to take her on their planned vacation. He had thought she wasn't like that, obsessed with material things, but he was starting to think maybe he never really knew her. Carl decided tomorrow would be a new day and everything will be better with her phone call in the morning.

The next morning came and went. So did lunchtime, but there was no call from Pauline. He tried calling her and there was no answer. He started to think the worst had happened, that she had fallen down the big staircase in her house and was lying there, dead, because of a broken neck.

He decided to jump in his car and check on her. When Carl pulled in the driveway, he noticed her neighbor's house, a huge Victorian like her's, was for sale. He recognized the realtor that was showing the home to a couple with three kids as Michael Constance, the man who had sold Marjorie's house for him. They smiled and waved at each other before Carl rang Pauline's door.

It took a moment before she moved the curtains in the window of the door to see who was outside. When she saw it was Carl, she unlocked the door but didn't' open it wide enough for him to come in.

"Pauline. I'm glad you are okay. I was worried."

Pauline laughed, just like Carl remembered her doing. "Why are you worried?"

"You said you would call this morning it's three o'clock and you never called or answered my phone calls. I thought you were dead."

Pauline looked at him and smiled. She then stepped out on to the porch, pulled the door closed behind her, and walked over to their swing. She patted gently on the seat for Carl to sit next to her.

"Carl, look. I've been doing some thinking. We had a great run together. I have made so many happy memories with you. Ones that I will treasure for as long as I have left. But the fact is, I think we need to move on. Go our separate ways."

Blood started to rush into Carl's ears, making his hearing go away and leaving only the sound of a jet engine in its place.

"What happened, Pauline? I thought we were happy together. I was planning our future. I was going to ask you to marry me this summer."

Pauline gently placed her hand on Carl's shoulder and smoothed out the sleeve of his checked shirt.

"I'm sorry."

She leaned over and gently gave him a kiss on the cheek before she got up, went into her house, and locked the door behind her.

Carl sat on the swing, the swing they had watched so many sunsets together, in shock. The birds chirped around him and the warm autumn breeze gently blew. Everything seemed normal, even though his world was crashing down.

He watched as the realtor ushered the family to their car and gave them a hardy wave goodbye.

Carl stood up and somberly walked to his car.

"Mr. Winston! It's so nice to see you again," said Michael walking over with his hand outstretched.

"Hi," said Carl trying to plaster a fake smile on his face to hide his true feelings.

"I wanted to thank you for letting me sell your house. People found out about what a great deal I got for you, the deal of a lifetime some say, and now everyone is requesting me to sell their houses."

Michael gave him a gentle pat on the back as they both walked to the sidewalk.

"I'm glad I could help," he said looking at the realtor.

"This house here," he said pointing to the Victorian next to Pauline's. "It's because of you. They decided to agree with me and list it higher at $405,000. Can you believe it? And this family I just showed it to, they are going to put in a full price offer."

Carl looked at Michael and smiled he didn't want to burst his bubble. There was no reason for two people to be unhappy.

"That is wonderful news, Michael. Congratulations," said Carl. "If you will excuse me, I need to head home."

The two men waved goodbye and returned to their respective cars.

That afternoon, Carl drove home. He wasn't sure how he even got there because he was so distracted. Once again, he ate a frozen dinner alone and went to bed with his head swirling.

He went back and forth about what could have changed Pauline's mind about him, and the only thought he had was about money. She loved him when he was rich, but now the money was gone, and she wanted nothing to do with him.

Carl didn't leave the house for days. He would move only from his bed, to the couch, to the kitchen, and back. He wasn't taking visitors. He wanted to remain alone.

A week had passed since he last spoke to Pauline. He decided he had to get closure from her.

He picked up the phone and dialed the number he knew so well.

"Hello," answered the voice on the other end.

Carl almost stopped breathing when he heard her.

"It's Carl," was all he could croak out. "I have been thinking about us since we ended things a week ago. Could you do me one last favor?"

There was a long pause.

"What is it?"

"Can we have dinner at your home one last time. I feel like I need some closure. After tonight, I promise to never bother you again."

There was a pause again.

"I don't know, Carl. This probably isn't a good idea."

"Please."

Silence.

"Alright, come here at 6 p.m. Sharp."

"I'll be there."

Carl showed up at the old Victorian that he had known so well, for what seemed like the last supper for his and Pauline's relationship.

He rang the door and smiled at her when she opened it. While she didn't look as thrilled to see him as he did her, she graciously took the lilies from him, just like she did on their first date, and put them in water.

"Thank you for this, Pauline," he said while stepping into her house.

She nodded and closed the door behind him and motioned toward the dining room.

The two sat in silence enjoying a roasted chicken with mashed potatoes and Brussels sprouts.

Finally, Carl decided to break the tension.

"What was it?"

Pauline put her fork down and gently dabbed the edge of her mouth with her napkin.

"What was what?"

"What was the reason you end things?"

Pauline mulled it over in her head before she answered.

"I feel we both wanted different things in our relationship," she said while absentmindedly swirling the red wine around in her glass. "You said it yourself, you wanted marriage, and I was looking for someone to spend time with and go on an adventure. Nothing more. I had done the marriage thing once and been tied down for many years. I feel like this is my time to explore and live my own life with the little time I have left."

Carl pushed around a Brussels sprout on his plate before putting down his fork.

"I can see that. I understand," he took a swig of wine. "Thank you for telling me. I feel like I will be able to move on now."

He reached out and gently squeezed her hand.

She returned his smile.

"But before you leave how about a slice of chocolate cake."

"I would love that, but only if you let me clear the dishes and serve it. You have been on your feet all day, it's the least I could do to say thank you," he said standing up.

"Carl, I insist. Let me do it."

"No, Pauline. Remember, my Momma raised me to be a gentleman," he said stacking all the plates and taking them into the kitchen.

Pauline finally gave in and relaxed at her seat in the dining room, while Carl rinsed the dishes, loaded them into the dishwasher, and prepared the chocolate cake and coffee.

After a few moments, Carl carried in a silver tea tray with two cups of coffee, a coffee pot, cream and sugar bowl, two large slices of chocolate cake, forks, and spoons.

"That was really not necessary, Carl. I could have done it. After all, you are my guest."

"No problem. It's just I'm used to helping you, and well, old habits, you know."

Pauline looked up at him and smiled. It was the same warm smile that Carl had grown to love.

They prepared their coffee in silence. The spoon gently tapping the side of the bone china giving it a gentle "tink" here and there. Then they both picked up their forks and started to enjoy the chocolate cake.

The heavenly dark cocoa rolled over their tongues and sweetened the backs of their throats.

Carl was thoroughly enjoying the cake when suddenly, Pauline dropped her fork. A blank look came over her face and she started to blink rapidly as her mouth opened wide.

"Is everything alright, Pauline?" he asked while looking over at her.

She slowly turned her head toward him as she threw her arms up and gripped her wrinkled fingers around her throat. Water started to pool in her eyes as the breath was caught in her lungs.

Crimson started to creep into her usually pale skin as she fought violently to catch her breath. Her chest was heaving up and down, trying in vain to produce air.

Carl picked up his napkin and dabbed gently at the corners to wipe away any rogue chocolate, then he walked carefully over to Pauline.

He grabbed her under the arms and lifted her out of the chair. She released one hand from around her neck, and grabbed onto the tablecloth, pulling everything including the china, coffee, and cake onto the floor.

Carl laid her half on the ground and half on his lap. He gently stroked her hair as she lay there starting to seize, while he remained perfectly calm.

"There now, Pauline. Go easy. It will be over soon. Shh," he said, treating her like a wounded animal.

She looked over at him with a mixture of shock, sadness, and agony as she laid there unable to breathe or speak a word. Water was streaming from her eyes, and drool was starting to come out of the corners of her mouth.

"You should have just kept things the way they were. We were good together. We were happy together. But now, you left me broke and alone. But I found a way to fix things. It's a shame I had to taint your delicious chocolate cake with poison. The poison you kept in your own kitchen."

Pauline looked right into Carl's eyes. The same eyes that she watched countless sunsets with. But now all the light was gone, and nothing but darkness was left.

In her final gasps, she thought about her life and all the things she would no longer get to do, and how a man she had loved, and then grew apart from, was the one putting an end to everything.

Pauline then went limp. Her body lost all of its rigidity and she lay motionless on the ground with her head in Carl's lap. Her cold, dead, eyes stared at the ceiling, and her mouth lay agape, no more breath coming out.

"Goodnight, darling," said Carl as he gave her a kiss on the forehead before gently lowering her off his lap and on to the floor.

He calmly got up, walked into the living room, and dialed 9-1-1.

"I need help. I think my friend is dead."

A week had passed since the death of Pauline O'Claira.

Because she had no living relatives an autopsy wasn't ordered, Carl's secret laid hidden so he could play the grieving boyfriend left behind.

Pauline was a private person about her relationships, so she never told anyone that she and Carl had called it off, not even her sewing circle friends, so everyone was heartbroken for the old man who had lost the second love of his life in under two short years.

Once again, Carl was called into an attorney's office and told he was the sole beneficiary of Pauline's estate, which was a pretty hefty sum. Something he was counting on.

Three days after she was buried, Carl was meeting with Michael Constance on the front porch of Pauline's house.

"I'm so sorry to hear about everything, Mr. Winston."

"Thank you, Michael. That's very kind of you. What do you think would be a fair asking price for the house?"

Michael paused and looked at the notes he had from the walk through he had done earlier.

"Since we got the full asking price for the house next door recently, and this one is a little bigger, I'm thinking we aim high and ask about $425,000. Do you think that's fair?"

Carl smiled.

"Oh yes. Quiet fair."

Summer came and Carl and his friend Eddie had a wonderful time on their fishing trip to Alaska. And since he was able to sell Pauline's house for the full asking price, he upgraded their airplane tickets and accommodations to first class.

He used some of the money to add on a section of his house to create a den with a floor to ceiling, stone fireplace.

Life was good, but he could see that the money he received from Pauline was going to start running out soon if he didn't slow down.

He pushed this thought from his mind as he headed back to Smithton's Market to once again stock up with enough supplies to make it through another week.

Carl pushed a shopping cart up and down the aisles gathering the mundane items like dish soap, laundry detergent, and swiss cheese. When he went to reach for a loaf of bread, he bumped hands with another person.

Carl looked over and saw an older woman with dark, black hair cut into a bob looking at him smiling.

"I'm sorry. I guess we have the same great taste," she said sharing a smile.

"We must," said Carl returning the gesture.

With dark green eyes sparkling, the woman held out her hand.

"I'm Loretta," she said.

"I'm Mr. Winston."

# Return to Sender

Jonas Emmerson took off his hat and name badge and threw them into the back of his car. His light brown hair that was starting to be bleached by the summer sun, was matted to his head with sweat.

He slammed the door, walked to the driver's seat and sat down happy to be done for the day. The sweat he accumulated throughout the day soaked through his shirt and made it cling to his chest and underarms. Although he wouldn't be considered overweight, or pudgy, the few extra pounds he carried on his frame made moving around in the heat a little more uncomfortable.

Jonas gripped the hot steering wheel that had been baking in the sun all day while throwing his head back against the seat.

"If I have to tell one more brat and overbearing parent what time the three o'clock parade starts, I am going to punch Sammy the Seal in the face."

He leaned forward and cranked up the AC as high as it would go. Unfortunately, the only thing he was greeted with was a blast of hot air as the car struggled to cool the air.

Jonas couldn't wait to get home from a long day working at Lakewood Amusement Park, "Home of everyone's favorite seal mascot, Sammy!"

The crowds, loud kids, and pushy parents made it a nightmare for him. If his parents hadn't forced him to take a summer job, then he wouldn't have been one of the front counter workers at "Sammy's Seafood on a Stick Shack." The smell of the seafood combined with the odor from fryers that haven't had the oil changed since Obama had been president, the first time, churned his stomach. It could also be the fact that his dad got sick on clams at the beach and wouldn't stop throwing up for twenty-four hours. Either way, this job was Jonas' idea of Hell.

The low rumble of his green hand-me-down Subaru Wagon meant freedom to Jonas. As he threw it in reverse and hit the gas, he had his first taste of independence since working his twelve-hour shift.

Luckily, it was only a ten-minute drive home for Jonas. He lived on Mountain Laurel Street with his mom, dad, and little brother Benjamin.

His father, Justin, did freelance video work, which would often take him out of town on business. Jonas had his suspicions on what "business" his father was doing while he was away but kept those ideas to himself.

His mother, Sara, worked as an editor for Carnaby Publishing. A well-known giant in the publishing world that was responsible for New York Times bestsellers such as "Carly's Nightmare," which was written by an author local in Seraphim Falls.

Jonas' parents decided to leave their New York City life just this past year, and move into a huge, Victorian house in Seraphim Falls. The house was beautiful with its light gray siding and teal trim and shutters. It even had a stained-glass window depicting a sprig of Mountain Laurel above the large bay window in the dining room.

According to his parents, the reason for moving was to provide Jonas and Benji with a better environment to grow up in, one away from dangerous city life. But Jonas suspects they needed to escape parts of their past they would rather soon forget.

As Jonas pulled into the driveway of his house, he waved to his next-door neighbor, Ms. O'Claira. She was a nice older lady, who was a little on the weird side. He always thought little, old, ladies should be at church bake sales and crocheting on the front porch, not going off on hunting trips and doing morning yoga in the backyard.

But he liked her and thought she made some of the best chocolate cake.

Half paying attention when he was pulling into the driveway, Jonas had to slam on his breaks just in time.

"Damn it, Benji!" he yelled.

Right in the middle of where Jonas was going to pull the car were three bicycles, thrown carelessly on their sides.

Jonas got out of the car and yelled "Benji" hoping his ten-year-old brother, or one of his friends, would hear him.

The car continued to idle in the driveway, with Jonas growing more agitated by the minute, until a boy, medium in height with unruly brown hair and freckles across the bridge of his nose came bounding around the side of the house with two other boys in tow.

"Move it!" yelled Jonas while jabbing his finger toward the bikes.

"Calm down. Don't get your panties in a bunch," said Benji as he and his friends picked up their bikes and pushed them into the yard.

"Was that so hard, Nerd?" asked Jonas as he got back in the car and shut the door behind him.

Benji made a face at his brother and stuck out his tongue in protest before he and his friends ran to the backyard again.

Jonas drove his car up, turned it off, and pulled out his phone.

Jonas: Dude. Dun with Hell. Coming Over?

A minute passed before he received:

Adam: Y. B over in 5.

Jonas put the phone in his pocket, got out of the car, and went inside his house.

He walked into the kitchen and helped himself to a can of Coke in the fridge and one of the homemade chocolate chips his mom made that morning. No matter how busy she was, Jonas could always count on his Mom to have fresh baked goods around.

On his way up the large staircase that boasted carvings of various leaves, Jonas played one of his favorite games. The second and tenth steps on the staircase always creaked. He liked to challenge himself to see if he could step on them with making noise. Unfortunately, just like yesterday, they groaned under his weight and Jonas lost his own game.

*One and five. I'll have to try harder next time.*

When he got to the top of the stairs, Jonas turned left and knocked on the door to his mom's office.

"Come in," said a muffled voice on the other side of the door.

Jonas put the cookie in his mouth, turned the doorknob with his free hand, and walked in.

His mother was sitting at her desk that was stacked high with papers and littered with cups of coffee in various states of emptiness. She was furiously typing away at her computer and held up one finger to motion for Jonas to wait one moment for her to finish and then she would talk to him.

When she stopped typing, she let out an exasperated sigh, turned to her son, and gave him a big smile.

"How was work today?"

"It was wonderful! Another day in paradise at Lakewood Amusement Park," he said while rolling his eyes.

"I'm sorry, honey. Just think, summer will be over soon and then you will be rid of that place."

"Yeah. Only because I'm back at school."

His mom laughed.

"You have such a hard life for a seventeen-year-old. Wait until you become an adult."

Jonas rolled his eyes. He always hated how adults made it seem like it was so hard being a grown-up and teens had it so easy.

Sensing the tension, Sara changed the subject.

"Is Adam coming over?"

"Yeah. He is supposed to be here any minute. I should probably go and change."

He said goodbye to his mom and went to his room to change out of his uniform in the hopes of no longer smelling like the catch of the day.

"Dude! We need to find something better than that," said Adam laying on his back, on Jonas' bed, tossing a football in the air and catching it while Jonas sat on his desk with his feet on the chair.

The two actually met at Lakewood Amusement Park. Jonas was doing his regular shift when Adam stopped a bunch of kids from being jerks and making a mess out of the condiment dispensers. Jonas went to thank him and the two talked for a while about their love of You Tube and the ideas they had for a channel. Since then, they had become great friends, Jonas' only one since moving here a few months ago. His friendship with Adam was probably the only good thing to come out of his job at the amusement park.

Now they were hanging out in Jonas' bedroom that was a separate wing from the rest of the second floor. His parents had let him pick the room because they felt bad, they were tearing him away from his life in New York City.

Not only did he like the privacy it allowed, but he liked the navy blue and burgundy plaid wallpaper and dark hardwood floors. It went along well with the navy-blue comforter on his bed, and the shelf along the top of the room. It was the perfect place for him to display some of the track trophies he had earned at his last school and a few framed posters of Jackson Pollock's work he saw when he used to visit the Guggenheim.

"We did the ghost pepper challenge, and then jellybean roulette. We need something big since we just hit a million subscribers," he said looking at Adam.

Silence hung in the room with only the thumping of the football hitting Adam's hands.

Jonas ran his fingers through his hair in fruition, while Adam put down the football, to take off his orange-brown glasses to clean the lenses with his t-shirt.

Suddenly Jonas' head snapped up.

"I saw a couple of other You Tubers doing this, and it has been popular," said Jonas turning around to sit in the chair so he could use the computer.

He turned on the monitor and typed in the video streaming website while Adam walked over toward the desk.

Jonas clicked on a video, "What you do is you buy a mystery box off the dark web. You have no idea what you are getting. Then you open it on camera. People go nuts over it. It's the perfect blend of mystery and danger."

Jonas and Adam watched as the guy in the video went to the front door to pick up his package.

In the background of the video, music that seemed to heighten the tension played as he grabbed the box and brought it to his kitchen table.

Adam and Jonas leaned closer to the monitor as a knife glided along the top of the box splitting the tape in half. Tension hung in the room as they waited to see what was inside.

"What are you doing, nerds? Watching people play with dolls online?"

Benji had opened the door to Jonas' room, allowing the door to slam into the wall, making a loud noise that caused Jonas to jump and Adam's bleach blond hair that was already spiked all over the place, stand even more on end.

"Ever hear of knocking, jerk?" said Jonas as he launched a pillow at his brother's head.

"Mom said dinner's ready and you need to come and eat," said Benji turning around, and running down the steps.

Disappointed Adam and Jonas turned back to the monitor.

"I'm going to head out, man. I think it's a good idea for a video. Let's try filming it tomorrow. We can film us buying it," said Adam standing up, grabbing his bag and heading out the door.

"One problem," said Jonas. "How are we going to get on the Dark Web?"

"Don't worry about it. I know someone, " said Adam.

The next day, when Jonas got home from another shift at Lakewood, Adam was waiting for him in his room.

"Hey! Your mom let me in and gave me these. I think I might move in," said Adam holding up a plate of homemade sugar cookies.

Jonas laughed and dropped his messenger bag on the floor near his bed, walked over, and grabbed a cookie.

"While I was waiting for you, I think I found our site," said Adam swiveling in the chair and placing his fingers on the keyboard.

"You know Brent in third period geometry?"

Jonas nodded, "The stoner?"

"Yep. The same. He gave me this site and said it would have what we were looking for."

Jonas rolled his eyes. He wasn't sure if he should trust the guy who is most likely to smoke oregano thinking it was weed.

Adam looked at the slip of paper and typed in the web address and hit enter as Jonas pulled over another chair so he could see the monitor better.

A black screen with a gray box asking for a password appeared.

Adam flipped the paper over and typed the website's password into the box and hit enter again.

The screen dissolved and went blank.

"See. I knew we shouldn't trust that pothead," said Jonas leaning back in the chair and crossing his arms in disgust.

Suddenly, the screen flashed to life and what looked like an eight-bit market stall with a blue striped awning came on the screen. A little, pixelated man dressed as a carnival barker with a red and white striped jacket and straw hat walked over from the left side.

A speech bubble over his head popped up that read "What are you looking for?"

Jonas and Adam stared at the screen still not believing they had hacked their way into the Dark Web.

"Dude, grab the camera. We need to film," said Jonas pointing across the room to where their equipment was stored.

Adam hopped up, grabbed the camera and tripod and set up a shot that included Jonas and the monitor in the frame. He then gave Jonas a Bluetooth mic to wear so his voice would be on the video too.

"I'll count you off," said Adam as he held up three fingers, then two, and one.

"What's up, fans and welcome back to 'The Bro Show.' I'm Jonas and Adam is behind the camera today."

Adam put his hand in front of the lens and waved.

"You liked our past challenges, so today we have the granddaddy of all challenges for you. You may have seen a few floating around on You Tube, but today you will have the opportunity to see, from start to finish, us buying a mystery box from the Dark Web."

"Cut," yelled Adam. "I'll hook the camera to the computer, and we can capture all of your movements online. That way it won't look terrible trying to shoot the screen."

Jonas moved out of the way, as Adam climbed under the desk, to hook up the camera to the computer tower. He put a mic on himself and sat next to Jonas.

"Just talk through everything as you do it," said Adam. "Ready when you are."

"Okay. Now you can see the screen and we'll have an up-close look at what we are doing.

"Before we started recording, we went to the website that we got from a buddy with connections, and we typed in the password. We wanted to keep that part confidential because things could get dangerous."

Jonas hit the refresh button and the market stall showed up again. The carnival barker walked out asking them what they wanted.

"So, what are we actually looking for?" asked Adam.

"I'm not sure. I guess we should have thought about this, huh," said Jonas as he gently tapped the keyboard with his nails.

"How about this?" asked Adam while he leaned over Jonas, took the wireless keyboard, and typed "mystery box."

The avatar on the screen then turned into a red genie with a puff of smoke. A new speech bubble came up and the words "as you wish" appeared. The image on the screen dissolved into falling pixels and went black.

Jonas and Adam looked at each other.

A bright flash happened, and then what looked like an old-school message board appeared.

"Alright! Looks like we're in, folks. Let's see what the Dark Web has to offer," said Jonas, taking the keyboard from Adam and placing it on the desk in front of him.

He pushed the down arrow to scan through the listings. It looked like there could be thousands of them.

Everything said the same thing, "mystery box" with the same exact description that read "a surprise delivered to your door. Outcomes vary. Nothing guaranteed."

"Everything looks identical," said Adam leaning closer to the screen.

Jonas took his mouse to the top of the page where there was a filter option. He opened it and chose "sort by price."

"How much do you want to spend, man?" he asked Adam.

"Twenty bucks?"

"That seems a little too cheap. How about fifty?" said Jonas.

They both agreed and scrolled down the message board until they got to the fifty-dollar listings.

There were twenty listings in the fifty-dollar price range. Still, each one titled the same thing with the same description. The only difference was the seller's names.

"Alright. Pick a number between one and twenty," said Jonas.

"Sixteen."

Jonas took the mouse over to the box in front of the sixteen and clicked it.

It opened a new window that asked for payment and mailing details.

"We'll cover this up, so people won't get our account information," Adam said as Jonas used the card that was connected to their YouTube account to purchase the box.

"Looks like we should be getting a package from the seller 'The Dark Architect' in a few days. Hold tight, boys and girls, and we promise it will be worth your while," said Jonas.

"That's a wrap for today," said Adam as he switched off the camera and began unhooking the equipment. "I guess all we have left to do is wait."

Jonas continued to work at his job at Lakewood. Every day when he came home, he looked anxiously for the package to arrive.

When it reached a week since ordering and the package still wasn't there, Jonas started to think they had been taken for a ride. That "The Dark Architect" had just stolen their money. The worst part was they couldn't do anything about it. What were they going to tell the police? "Officer, I would like to report that someone on the Dark Web took my money and failed to deliver the mystery package that I had ordered."

It had been a horrible day at work for Jonas. The heat had made everyone more demanding than usual, and he felt fried just like the food he made all day.

One month had passed since he ordered the package and was surprised when he walked into his family's kitchen after work to see a box sitting on the island.

"That came for you," said his dad nodding his head toward the brown paper package, held together with brown tape and red twine.

Jonas approached the island and saw his name and address written on it in hurried letters scrawled with a black Sharpie.

His heart dropped into his stomach. He never expected it to show up at all, but now, here it was.

Jonas gingerly picked up the box that was roughly the size of a toaster and looked underneath. He wasn't sure what he was looking for but was glad to see it wasn't stained or wet.

*I guess I can check off dead animals or human organs from the list of suspected objects.*

Jonas tucked the box under his arm and went to his room. He put it on the desk, picked up his phone, and texted Adam.

Jonas: Come over now. Box here

A few moments passed before he received a text back.

Adam: On my way.

It was the longest ten minutes Jonas had ever experienced. While he waited, he turned the box over in his hands. It didn't feel heavy. He could hear things rattling around inside. He hoped nothing had broken, because then everything would be a bust.

Jonas' door flew open, but it wasn't who he was expecting to see.

"I hear you got a package today. Could it be the rest of your brains that you lost," said Benji walking into the room and flopping down on the bed.

"Get lost," said Jonas, only half paying attention to his brother.

"No, seriously. What is it? It looks pretty cool," said Benji getting up and walking over to touch the package.

"It's none of your business," said Jonas lightly pushing him away. "It's for something Adam and I are working on."

Benji stood there with his arms crossed and a scowl on his face.

At that moment Adam walked in, huffing and puffing like he had run all the way to Jonas' house.

"It came. I can't believe it came. Here I thought we got ripped off. I figured the first time we went on the Dark Web we would have gotten ripped off," he said walking over to the package and picking it up to look at it.

"Dude? What the hell?" said Jonas pointing to Benji standing right there.

Adam hadn't seen Jonas' brother standing in the room.

Benji's eyes got wide as he looked between the two older boys.

"You bought something from the Dark Web? That's so cool! Now I have to see what's inside," he said taking a seat on the bed.

"Nope. Get lost. This is for You Tube," said Jonas standing up and picking up his little brother under his arms to kick him out of the room.

"If you don't let me stay, I'm going to tell Mom and Dad you are doing illegal things."

Jonas stopped. He really didn't want to get in trouble with his parents. He couldn't afford to be grounded let alone have his You Tube account taken away.

He put his brother back down in the room and shut the door. He bent down and put his face right in front of Benji's, their noses almost touching, and gave his kid brother a threatening look.

"You breathe a word of this to Mom and Dad I'll kill you. You have to sit on that bed and not say a word. Do you understand me?"

Benji pushed his brother away and flopped on the bed.

"Of course, I do. I ain't no narc."

Jonas shut and locked the door to his room, while Adam rushed around closing all the blinds and curtains to make everything dark.

While Adam was pulling over a small table to the middle of the room, Jonas turned on a few floor lamps that created a spooky, midnight society, vibe.

Adam checked the viewfinder on the camera, that he had set up on a tripod, to make sure the lighting was alright. He gave Jonas a thumbs up as he was putting the package on the table.

"Let me get us mic'd up and then we can take our seats and start," said Adam.

After they were both fitted with their mics, and Jonas shot a warning look at Benji, Adam began rolling and took his seat next to Jonas.

"It's been about a month, but we finally got it. We got our suspicious package from "The Dark Architect," said Jonas deepening his voice at the end to make it sound foreboding.

"Remember, we have no idea what's inside. We paid fifty bucks, gave them our address, and they shipped it to us," said Adam.

Picking up the package Jonas said, "As you can see it looks like an ordinary, brown paper wrapped package with red twine. You ready to open this thing?"

"Let's do it, "responded Adam.

Jonas sat the package down and reached for the scissors that were on the table next to the box. He first cut the top of the red twine, that fell to the sides once the tension was broken.

He found the middle of the box and opened the scissors, so they were more like a blade. Jonas pushed the tip through the center of the top. It made a snapping sound letting him know he broke through the tape.

Jonas slid the scissors along the top and across the sides freeing the box flaps and allowing it to open.

Adam helped him bend the flaps toward the sides of the box.

"We have it open, but inside, all we can see is some brown packaging paper," said Jonas tilting the box for the camera.

Benji was leaning off the bed trying to see inside of the box.

"Here is what we have been waiting for, folks. The moment of truth," said Jonas as he began to take the paper out.

Adam grabbed the camera off the tripod and brought it over with him to shoot down into the box, while Benji quietly slithered off the bed to see what was inside.

Once about ten pieces of crumbled up brown paper were removed, the mystery was no longer.

Inside was a black and white photo and what appeared to be an old, rubber, doll head.

"That, ladies and gentlemen, is what getting duped looks like. We paid fifty bucks for an old photo and doll head," said Jonas as he took the contents out of the box and held them up for the camera to see.

"Lame!" said Benji, which caused Jonas to shoot him daggers.

Adam returned the camera to the tripod as Jonas put the photo and doll head on the table.

"The picture is of two women working on what appears to be doll heads in a factory somewhere," said Jonas as Adam zoomed in on the photo.

Jonas turned the doll head around in his hands. The chubby cheeks modeled plastic hair that came to the top in a swirl, and the white vacant eyes seemed to mock him.

"Let this be a lesson, never buy another stranger's crap."

"Cut," yelled Adam.

"What the actual hell? I can't believe I wasted fifty dollars on this crap. Now we have a super lame video. What are we going to do?" said Jonas as he put the photo and doll down and ran his fingers through his hair in frustration.

"Ha. Right. Like all of your other videos aren't lame. Later losers," said Benji as he ran out of the room, slamming the door behind him.

Adam began to put all of the equipment away.

"You know what? I'll ask my grandpa. He has lived here his whole life, and if he has a good day, he might remember something," he said while coiling the camera's cable and putting it away in the hard sided case. "We are supposed to visit him at the nursing home tonight, so I can ask him then," Adam explained.

Jonas nodded his approval. He was only half paying attention because he was looking at the doll again. There was something about its knowing smile that left him unsettled.

"I'm heading out man. See you tomorrow after work?" asked Adam.

"Uh, yeah," said Jonas absentmindedly, disappointment clouding his brain. "See you then."

The day seemed to drag on for Jonas.

It was another scorcher and working around fried food made it even hotter. Even the smell of grease and seafood started to make him nauseous.

Jonas leaned over the counter and wiped the sweat off his forehead with the inside of his shirt.

Just as he was turning to get a cup of ice water from the dispenser, he heard a loud "Excuse Me!"

Jonas rolled his eyes, set down the cup, and turned around with a fake smile plastered on his face.

"How can I help you, ma'am?"

The woman, who looked less than thrilled standing with her hands on her hips and head cocked to one side said, "My son said the men's bathroom around the corner is an awful mess."

"I will let our custodians know right away."

"I'm afraid that isn't good enough. You need to take care of it right now. I want to speak to your manager."

The woman had said the exact phrase every service worker rolls their eyes at.

Hearing the angry woman over the din of children laughing on a nearby ride and people placing their food orders, Jonas' manager, Marcus, came over.

"Is there a problem here?"

"I was just telling your employee the bathroom around the corner is an absolute mess and it needs to be cleaned right away."

"We apologize for that and we will take care of it right away. Here, take this coupon and have a free Sammy's Fish Sammie on us."

He handed her the coupon that seemed to satisfy her as she walked away and joined up with the eight-year-old boy that must have found the mess.

"You heard what you have to do," said Marcus turning toward Jonas.

"But I'm not the custodian."

"It needs to be taken care of right away, so you take care of it."

Marcus turned and went to the back of the kitchen to continue to expedite the food.

Jonas groaned, took off his apron, and went out the side door.

He stopped at the janitor's storeroom to pick up cleaning supplies and then headed to the restroom.

Not knowing what to expect, Jonas donned rubber gloves and a face mask before he stepped into the bathroom.

Jonas' jaw dropped as he saw the woman wasn't kidding. There were brown paper towels all over the floor and toilet paper was thrown over the tops of the stalls. The smell that came from the place was awful. It was a combination of something that was sickeningly sweat mixed with a more earthy scent. The heat of the day was causing it to be stronger than it would have been on its own. Jonas gaged a few times. He wasn't sure what he hated worse, the seafood shack or this bathroom.

He groaned and began to take down the toilet paper and put in the trash can he brought with him.

As Jonas bent down to pick up the crumpled paper, he saw something was hiding underneath.

He bent down, looked closer, and saw it was something red. It seemed thick and sticky and clung to the paper towels when he picked them up.

Jonas dropped the paper towel and jumped back. The goo was a dark red color and looked like blood.

Drawing in all of his courage Jonas looked again, getting even closer. This time he smelled the air around the red mass. Instead of the usual metallic smell that accompanies blood, this smelled sweet.

"Damn it!" said Jonas breathing a sigh of relief. "It's ketchup."

Jonas bent down and picked up the rest of the paper towels.

Once they were off the floor, he stood back and looked at what was left. Instead of seeing a massive blob, there was something written.

Jonas stood up as his face went white. His knees began to feel weak when he pulled out his phone to take a photo of the floor and text it to Adam.

"Dude, this is really creepy."

"How do you think I feel? It happened where I worked, and it has my name in it."

The two of them were sitting in Jonas' room later that evening.

"Let's pull the photo up on your computer and get a better look at it," said Adam pulling a chair next to Jonas at the desk.

Jonas typed in his password information to access the cloud where all of his photos were stored. He clicked on the folder marked with today's date and double clicked on the photo.

The photo was enlarged to take up the entire screen. Written on the bathroom floor, in ketchup made to look like blood was, "Jonas, find the rest of me."

"What could this mean? Find the rest of the bottle," asked Adam leaning back in the chair, lacing his hands behind his head.

Jonas shot him a look. "Why would someone want us to find the rest of the ketchup bottle? That's stupid."

"What if," said Jonas but he stopped talking as both boys looked at the screen.

Just like when they were logged on the Dark Web, the photo dissolved off the screen and nothing was left but darkness.

However, this time a new window opened on the web browser.

"What are you doing?"

"I'm not doing anything, Adam."

The boys leaned in closer as the same 8-bit market stall graphic appeared on the page.

"I'm definitely not doing this."

Out came the carnival barker and a speech bubble appeared over his head. This time he wasn't asking what they were looking for.

*Jonas, find the rest of me.*

After the bubble, the barker held out his hand and a pixelated head appeared in his palm.

Adam and Jonas looked at each other.

A loud knock on Jonas' door caused both of them to jump in their seats and turn around. The knob turned and Benji walked in with a box.

"Mom said for me to give this to you. Hey! Cool. Who is that guy? Is that a severed head? That's awesome," said Benji walking in and setting the box on the floor next to his brother.

Jonas reached down and picked up the box. It was wrapped in the same brown paper and red twine. The hurried handwriting in black marker was there, but the box was a little smaller.

When he shook it, Jonas could hear something rattling inside.

Adam went and grabbed the camera as Jonas reached into his side drawer to grab his scissors. After recording began, Jonas cut through the twine and tape as Adam and Benji peered inside with him.

The same brown packing paper was balled up, but once Jonas threw it on the floor, they could see there were about thirty doll heads inside. They wore the same vacant expression and dead white eyes.

"Sweet!" said Benji reaching for a head.

Jonas slapped his hand away and put the box on the floor. Adam kept recording while Jonas reached in and found the same photo of the women working on the doll heads. This time, written in red marker was "Jonas, come find me."

Jonas dropped the photo back in the box, tucked in the flaps, and rushed the package downstairs. He went straight through the kitchen and out the back door where he opened the trash can and shoved the box inside before slamming down the lid.

He paused for a moment to catch his breath and to let his adrenaline settle before he slowly walked back up the steps to his room.

"We need to put an end to this once and for all," said Jonas to Adam.

"I want to do it, too," said Benji springing up from his seat on the floor. "This is getting sick."

"Sorry. Mom would kill me if I dragged you into this."

Benji looked at Jonas with pain behind his eyes. He started to open his mouth to make some smart-ass comment but decided against it. Instead, he lowered his eyes to the floor, not wanting his brother to see the tears starting.

"You never want to hang out with me anymore. You just want to make your stupid videos with Adam," he said pushing past Jonas and walking into the hall.

"It isn't that at all. It's just too," Jonas couldn't finish his sentence before his brother slammed the door to his room.

"He'll get over it," said Adam. "You can make it up to him once we figure this out and you stop receiving creepy care packages in the mail."

Jonas shrugged and sunk down on his bed. He laid on his back and stared at the ceiling while Adam watched back the footage they had recorded when they went online to purchase the first package.

"Oh, I totally forgot," said Adam putting down the camera and going to Jonas' computer. "I talked to my grandfather last night about the photo. He was having a rough night, slipping in and out of it, but he did say the phrase 'doll factory fire'."

Jonas sat up in the bed, "Doll factory fire? I don't think I've ever heard about it."

"Well, since you are pretty new to Seraphim Falls you probably wouldn't have."

Adam typed a few things into a search engine and brought up a page that had information about the Castava Doll Factory Fire of 1942.

"I can't believe I forgot about this. Some of the old-timers still talk about it today."

Jonas scooted closer to the monitor and read about how in the summer of 1942 The Castava Doll company's main factory, located on the outskirts of Seraphim Falls, caught fire killing 200 people and injuring another 175. It was the biggest labor-related catastrophe in the entire country at the time.

He scrolled further down to read about the cause, but nothing was listed.

"No one knows for sure what caused it," said Adam as if reading Jonas' mind. "Some say it was an electrical fire or the chemicals used to make the plastic for the dolls reacted and caused an explosion. Others say it was arson."

Jonas turned to look at his friend. He didn't necessarily like the idea of traipsing around a burned-out warehouse at night, but he had to do something so all of the packages and messages would stop.

"I think we found where we need to go tonight."

It was later at night around 10 p.m. when Jonas got a text message.

Adam: Outside. Block away.

Jonas sent a quick message back to let him know he was on his way, before he sneaked out of the house with a camera, and into his car. His parents were pretty liberal about him leaving the house late at night, but he didn't think they would be okay with him going to an abandoned factory.

He drove to the end of the street, trying to coast the car as much as he could, where Adam was waiting at the corner for him.

"Bring all the equipment?" Adam asked as he slid into the passenger side of the wagon and shut the door.

"It's in the trunk. You sure you want to do this?"

"It's not that I necessarily want to do it. It's that we have to. Think of how many hits we are going to get on this video. People eat this stuff up," replied Adam.

The two continued the fifteen-minute drive to the outer edges of Seraphim Falls. They remained silent as the darkness laid out in front of them and the yellow lines on the pavement appeared and disappeared in the headlights.

They drove past the town's famous waterfall and continued until houses and open fields were replaced with thickly wooded areas on either side. Jonas stayed alert, watching for deer, as they wound down the twisty road.

When they rounded one of the corners of the road, Jonas saw a few streetlights illuminating what looked like a dark, massive skeleton of a structure. It seemed to be waiting in the darkness like a beacon beckoning people to come and do dark deeds.

"There it is. In all its glory," said Adam as Jonas slowly drove into one of the only open areas that weren't covered with massive plant growth. "Once we park, I want to get a few establishing shots."

Jonas turned off the car, and Adam got out of the car, shut the door and tapped on the trunk.

Jonas reached down and unlocked the hatch so Adam could get to the equipment. He then sat there for a moment; his hands frozen to the wheel.

He stared at the exposed beams that were rusted from years of being open to the elements, and he looked at what remained of the walls. With the little amount of light, he could see they must have turned black by the flames that consumed not just the structure but the lives of many people.

Vines, weeds, and even what looked like trees were starting to wind their way over the building, like nature was trying to take back the property that was theirs while also erasing this monument to a horrible tragedy that now lays in waste.

Jonas didn't think about it until now, but he and Adam were going to be walking on hallowed ground. This was the place where many people lost their lives, screaming in pain as they were burned to death.

"You ready to go in," said Adam bending down to Jonas' window, snapping him back to reality.

Jonas nodded and got out of the car. He shut the door and locked it. Adam gave him a look as if to say, *"Who do you think is going to steal your car, out here, at this time of night?"*

Jonas just shrugged him off.

As they got closer to the structure, Jonas noticed there was a fence around the property with no trespassing signs posted. It was too tall for them to hop it, plus the barbed wire deterred them from climbing it. Jonas wasn't sure if he was more relieved or disappointed that it seemed like they wouldn't be able to get in.

"Hey! Over here," said Adam as he pulled a bush away from the fence revealing a hole cut through the chain links big enough for them to fit through.

Adam handed the camera to Jonas and slipped through the fence. He then reached out his hands to take the camera so Jonas could follow through.

Once they were both on the inside, Adam started to fire up the camera.

"Do you want to do a stand-up and talk about what led us here," he said switching everything on and powering a light that was attached to the camera.

"Dude! No. Have some respect. Let's just record as we look around. I want to get in and out as fast as possible."

"Why? Are you scared," said Adam mocking him?

"No. I just don't like trying to sensationalize the place where a lot of people took their last breaths, that's all. So can we just go on?"

Adam sighed and followed Jonas.

Gravel and weeds crunched under their feet as they walked to the side of the building where there was a door.

Jonas reached out, pressed the button above the rusted handle, and pulled. Nothing happened. He pulled again. The door that was once a shade of blue had now turned white from the sun speckled with rust refused to budge.

In his frustration, he pounded his fist above the handle and made one last effort.

This time it gave away and opened with a rusty screech that Jonas was sure could be heard back in town. He looked at Adam, who just gave him a nod indicated that he should go inside.

Jonas grabbed a flashlight from his back pocket, pressed the button with a click, and poked his head inside.

The light shown as a narrow beam only illuminating a small section of the cavernous building at a time.

"This area, must not have been damaged too bad in the fire," said Jonas walking in with Adam following behind.

Broken glass glittered from the flashlight and the light from Adam's camera. Jonas aimed his light upward and saw what remained of windows high above what appeared to be a work area.

What Jonas guessed to be about ten workbenches were spread out evenly in the open room, and stools were scattered all around. Some were standing upright, while others looked like they had been knocked over in a hurry.

Adam and Jonas walked closer to the benches. They could see there was something laying all over them, but from this far away and with such limited light they had to get closer before they could tell they were various pieces of dolls. Plastic arms, legs, and torsos were thrown all over the surface. It looked like a plastic, cannibal's butcher shop.

"Cool!" said Adam as he walked closer to the workbench and picked up a few of the doll pieces and held them up to the camera.

"I guess we know where all of your creepy doll heads came from," he said.

Jonas looked on the table taking in the sight of all the random body parts lying there as if waiting for someone to come back and put them all together. Even though it was just plastic doll pieces, to Jonas, it felt wrong and even grotesque.

"Well, we found 'the rest of me'," he said backing away after having seen enough.

"That's it?" said Adam disappointed. "We came out here to find a table full of doll parts after receiving creepy messages and packages? That's all?"

"I guess," said Jonas half distracted by seeing what else was in the room.

He continued to shine his light around the room. Behind him, Jonas saw a row of what looked like lockers.

There were five total, and none of them had locks. He started at the right and worked his way down the line, opening doors as he went.

Inside, he didn't find much. An empty lunch pail, paint brushes, a uniform shirt, and a few tools.

When he opened the fifth, and final, locker, Jonas dropped his flashlight.

"You okay, dude," said Adam bringing the camera with him, while still recording.

Jonas bent down and picked up his flashlight and shone it at the back of the locker.

"Adam, look at this," he said while reaching to take down a black and white photo that was held in the back of the locker with a magnet.

"What is that?" asked Adam as he zoomed in on the photo with the camera.

They stared at a black and white photo that showed a hallway somewhere in the factory. It looked like any old hallway with peeling plaster and massive cobwebs above door jams.

But what made this place different were dark, black marks radiating outside of the double doors at the end of the hallway. These marks continued past all the doors on the sides until they disappeared out of the frame of the photo.

Above the double doors read a sign "chemical room."

Jonas flipped over the photo and written on the back in red marker was "Seek and you shall find."

"What the hell?" said Jonas looking at the photo of the hallway again. His hand starting to shake. "I'm out. This is going too far."

"Dude, I get it. I agree but hear me out. We have to continue. Think of all the ratings we'll get."

Jonas looked at Adam and threw the picture down on the ground.

"Is this all about ratings for you? Is that all you care about? People died here, Adam. And we might be next. This place is dangerous. Who knows when a chunk of the ceiling or wall might fall on us, or maybe we will fall through the floor. If you want to continue on, be my guest, but I'm out."

Jonas turned to walk away and knocked over a metal stool in frustration.

Adam looked at his friend leaving. He shut off the camera and sat it down on the workbench.

"Jonas, wait up," he said jogging up to his friend who had stopped and turned around.

"You're right. I've been selfish. I just get so wrapped up in our You Tube channel that I forget things are happening in the real world," he said. "You might find this hard to believe, but I'm not the most popular guy at school, and when we do these videos and get all the subscriptions and likes, it makes me feel like less of a loser. I'm sorry that I got caught up. You're right. This has gone far enough. We should leave. Let me grab the camera."

Jonas felt awful at how he treated Adam. He had no idea how Adam felt about their channel and what life was like for him at school.

"It's okay, man. Let's get out of here and forget about it," Jonas said while gently squeezing Adam's shoulder.

Adam went back to the workbench for the camera and then they walked to the door they used to come in. Jonas reached for the handle and pulled toward himself. Knowing how hard it was to open the first time, he pulled again. Nothing happened. He tried the same trick of pounding above the handle, and nothing happened.

"Here. Hold this," said Adam passing the camera to Jonas.

He tried four more times and it refused to budge.

"What are we going to do now?" asked Jonas.

"We are just going to have to find another way out," said Adam. "I'm going to click on the light on the camera so we can see better.

Jonas and Adam shone their lights around the room.

"Look over there," said Jonas spotting a door that led into another part of the defunct factory. "Want to give that a shot?"

"Looks like it's our only option."

The two of them shone their lights toward the door that was on the right side of the room as they carefully crossed over empty packing boxes.

When they reached the door, Jonas pushed down on the handle and it swung open easily, despite the few groans from the old door.

After stepping into the hallway, Jonas and Adam shone their lights around. They could see doors on either side of the hallway. Adam reached out to touch one that was closest to him and noticed they were made of wood and had heavy brass knobs. They were different than the other doors they had seen in the rest of the factory.

The doors weren't the only thing that was different about this part of the factory. The air felt strange. It seemed almost thicker like you almost had to drink it into your lungs in order to breathe.

Jonas swore he could almost taste something when he took a deep enough breath. It was something he had tasted before but couldn't put his finger on it. It reminds him of summer, and times he spent around family.

He kept trying to think of what it reminded him of as he shone his flashlight straight ahead down the hallway. The doors continued all the way in front of them into the darkness where they couldn't see what was beyond the reach of their lights.

"I'll take the left side and you take the right?" suggested Adam nodding to the doors at their sides.

"Sounds good to me."

The boys tried the doors on their designated sides and were disappointed to find none of them would open. They were either locked or swollen shut with age. Both Jonas' and Adam's hands were turning black from touching the doorknobs. It seems like their age was coming off in the boys' hands.

The air continued to get thicker, and the taste was growing deeper in Jonas' mouth.

After having no success trying about twenty doors the boys were at the end of the hallway.

They turned to talk to each other, and Jonas let out a gasp.

"I thought this place looked familiar. I started noticing it with the black all over the walls, and now with this, I know where we are."

Jonas backed up and shone his light above the doorway of the double doors at the end of the hall. It read "chemical room."

"Shit," said Adam at almost a whisper.

And it hit Jonas. He finally discovered the taste he had in the back of his throat. It tasted like charcoal on the grill. His chest began to tighten. This combined with the different air made Jonas start to feel lightheaded.

"We ended up right where they wanted us to," said Jonas with a shake in his voice.

"Look," said Adam trying to sound upbeat in order to prevent his friend from having a panic attack. "Maybe, whoever it was that sent us on this wild goose chase, had their fun and wanted to provide us with a way out. That is why they gave us the picture."

"I'm not sure. They did send us all these creepy doll heads, so they're really not right in the brain."

Jonas stood there, with the beam of his flashlight on the double doors, thinking about what to do next. The rational part of his brain began to take over, and he was able to slow his breathing. He tried to think of other possible ways out of this situation but couldn't come up with any.

"I guess we don't have many options," he said to his friend. "We might as well 'seek and find.'"

"Whatever you say, buddy. I'm right with you."

Jonas looked at his friend as they both smiled trying to summon enough courage to step into the great unknown.

Jonas reached out, his hand shaking, and pushed the lever down on the right-hand door. Just like the door to this hallway, it gave no resistance. He walked through with Adam following behind.

They both shone their flashlights around but couldn't see anything but blackness. It was a darkness that seemed to swallow everything they came in contact with.

There was no sound in the room either. Jonas couldn't hear the crickets outside, a distant hooting of an owl from the surrounding woods, or even an occasional car driving past.

All there was the thumping of his heart in his ears and the patter of his sneakers on the concrete.

"Adam, I don't like this. I think we made a mistake," said Jonas trying to back up while avoiding tripping over his own feet.

Out of the darkness came a deep, gravelly voice, that somehow sounded soothing at the same time.

"Thank you, Adam, for bringing me what I wanted."

# Redneck Rendezvous

"I told you we had no idea where we were going, Cassie," said a man in his early twenties with long dark hair that hung to just under his chin.

"Listen, Micah, I've been reading maps ever since I was going on road trips with my parents starting at age six."

Cassie angrily searched in her purse for a hair tie to pull back her straight auburn hair. This was something she always did when she felt like she was pushed to the limit.

Micah looked over at her and noticed the flush that was starting to form under the freckles that were appearing on the bridge of her nose. This was caused by the sunlight streaming through the windows hitting Cassie's sensitive, milky skin.

He sighed deeply. He hated making her feel like this. He reached his right hand over to her while keeping his left on the steering wheel and rubbed her knee as she stared out the window.

"Look I'm sorry," he said. "You just know how being lost makes me feel so anxious."

Cassie's expression softened. She changed her gaze from the window and looked over at Micah and squeezed his hand that was still on her leg.

"I know. I guess I was a little defensive," she said.

Thick trees and dark green brush roared past them as they wound their way through a back country road that looked like a huge black snake sunning itself before them.

Cassie picked up the map she had thrown down in frustration, smoothed it out, and tried to find their location.

She spent about twenty minutes before she said, "I quit. I have no clue."

Cassie threw up her hands in frustration. "We are in the middle of the woods, so it is near impossible to find out where we are. Let's do what you suggested. Let's use GPS."

Micah tried to hide a smile that was forcing its way onto his lips. He loved to be right, but not at the expense of his girlfriend.

"If you're sure," he said double-checking that Cassie wanted to give up on her personal quest.

That is what he loved most about her, her determination and strength. Life hasn't always been easy for her. Losing her brother when she was only ten years old, had a huge effect on her. But after seeking help she came out even stronger.

"Just pull over to the next open area we come across and we can plug the address into the car. Since this is a rental, I'm not sure how to use the system," said Cassie.

Micah nodded and kept an eye out for a place as they continued down the country road for another five miles until they came across what looked like an abandoned factory.

"There!" shouted Cassie as she pointed toward an area next to the blackened structure that twisted toward the sky like a long-dormant skeleton that took its secrets to its grave.

Micah turned the burgundy CR-V into the gravel path and put it in park.

Cassie pulled out her phone and opened up her memo app. She leaned over and punched the address into the screen.

"There. Now we should be on our way to Lakewood Amusement Park," she said excitedly as she leaned back in her seat. "We are finally going to see the place that was made famous in 'Carly's Nightmare.'"

Micah was equally excited. They both loved the book. It was actually how they met. They went to a book signing and ended up standing in line next to each other. They decided to have coffee afterward and now, here they were on their way to see the inspiration for the amusement park where Carly had been trapped.

Micah put the car in drive and turned onto the road.

They continued traveling. The conversation went from what attractions they wanted to check out when they got to Lakewood, what the perfect cheese for a burger was, and what was the ultimate 1980s kids movie.

Time passed quickly and daylight started to fade.

Cassie looked nervously out the window as Micah continued to follow the directions that were being called out by the disembodied voice of the GPS.

"Shouldn't we have been there by now?" asked Cassie as she nervously played with a rogue string on her jeans.

"I thought so, but this is still telling us where to go," said Micah indicating the car's console with his hand, not on the steering wheel.

"Maybe we should stop and ask someone for directions," said Cassie.

Micah sighed. He hated when technology failed him and hated it, even more, when he had to get help.

"Maybe the next place we pass we will ask."

Cassie's shoulders seemed to relax a little. She was happy Micah agreed to ask for directions without putting much of a fight.

The car continued for three more miles down a long-forgotten, forest road when they came across what could be called a convenience store in the loosest sense of the word.

Micah pulled off into the parking lot of the shack. It was made of weather-beaten boards that looked like they were built using kindergarten paste and a prayer. The roof had so many patches that it looked like a quilt, and the windows were so caked with years of mud and dust that it looked abandoned. If it wasn't for a sign on the door that read, "yes we're open," Micah wouldn't have known the place was still in business.

Micah turned off the car and turned toward Cassie.

"I'll be back in just a moment."

Cassie reached out and grabbed his arm.

"Wait! I'm getting a bad feeling about this. Maybe we can just skip finding the amusement park. Let's just do something else. I'm sure Seraphim Falls has other things to do."

"No. We came all this way to see Lakewood and we are going to see it," said Micah walking away angrily. Micah was starting to get annoyed with Cassie never wanting to take a chance on anything.

Cassie slumped into the seat and turned away from him as he slammed the door and walked toward the store.

Micah pulled open the store door and a little bell tinkled above. The gentle sound seemed so out of place with the rest of the surroundings.

There wasn't a whole lot inside. There were some prepackaged foods like potato chips and snack cakes, but Micah bet they were long past their expiration date.

Sitting on shelves were a few other convenience items like batteries, quarts of oil, and washer fluid. Micah ran his finger over them and saw the line in the thick coating he left behind.

He glanced behind the counter and was surprised to see a print of Picasso's "The Weeping Woman."

The store was so quiet except for a rusty table fan that moaned in the corner trying its best to keep the sticky, stagnant air moving around the room.

"What can I do ya for," said a deep voice with a long drawl behind Micah.

Micah's shoulders jumped as he was surprised to see someone standing behind the cash register. He swore the man wasn't there a moment ago.

"Hey man. Yeah. Um… nice taste in art," said Micah pointing to the wall where the framed print hung.

The man walked around Micah and went behind the counter, never taking his eyes off of him.

"I'm sure you didn't come in here to talk about my taste in art. Waddya want," he said with an edge to his voice.

Micah shifted uncomfortably for a moment. He hated dealing with confrontation.

"We are a little lost and I was hoping you could point me in the right direction."

The clerk, who looked to be between his late thirties and early forties stared unblinking at Micah. His beard clad mouth kept chewing something while his dark, brown eyes looked vacantly back at him.

Micah has guessed this guy's name was Steve because the patch on his dark, blue work shirt and matching hat had it stitched on.

Steve finally nodded in answer to Micah's question before he reached under the counter, grabbed an empty Mountain Dew bottle, and spit brown liquid into it.

Micah tried to hide his wincing at the disgusting habit. He changed his line of sight so Steve wouldn't see him. He looked down at the counter. It, like the rest of the store, was a mess and was littered with mail. A lot of it had the same sender in the top left corner, The Dark Architect.

"What ya do is you go down this road here for about four more miles and then make a left," he said while leaning forward and looking out the front window.

He stopped talking for a moment, as if something distracted him outside.

Steve turned his head back to Micah and gave him a big grin.

"She your girl?"

Micah shifted uncomfortably, "Yeah."

"You a lucky man. She really pretty."

Micah could see a look in Steve's eyes that he didn't like. He straightened up and squared his shoulders. "Back to the directions?"

The smile started to fade from Steve's face, like wax melting in the sun.

"Just continue straight and you'll run into it," he said leaning back, his face turning to stone.

Micah shifted uneasily for a moment before he turned to leave. He said thanks over his shoulder before he pushed on the door, causing the little bell to tinkle again.

His feet kicked gravel and dust as he walked to the CR-V, opened the door and sat down.

"That was a waste," he said slamming the door and starting the car.

Cassie looked over toward him. "What happened?"

"Let's just say we are better off with the GPS."

Cassie buckled herself in and looked back at the store. Through the dust and dirt that covered window, she could see a man standing there looking at her. A shiver went down her spine as she watched him until the car backed out and traveled down the road; the store disappearing from sight.

The sun began to set behind the trees as Cassie and Micah wound down the same road, they had been traveling all day.

"Okay. Only five more miles and we should be there," said Micah downward toward the GPS screen.

Cassie remained silent and stared out the window, her hand resting under her chin. She never liked technology and felt uneasy about it, especially when they were trusting it to lead them at night.

"Just right around the corner," said Micah. "Here we are."

"You have arrived at your destination," said the calm voice of the GPS.

But what Micah and Cassie saw made them anything but calm.

The forest that surrounded them on their drive gave way to a clearing. Sitting in the middle was what looked like a white farmhouse with a wrap-around porch. While it wasn't completely falling down, the home had seen better days. The white paint was starting to peel, and the windows seemed to have a permanent fog. An older looking truck sat in the gravel driveway. It mirrored the same look as the house, except it had rust peeling around the doors. But, despite the decrepit appearance, it seemed like the house was well kept with flowers in planters and lace curtains in front of warm table lamps in the windows.

As Micah and Cassie were staring up at the house, there was a loud rap on their door.

They jumped and looked over to see a man in his late 50s with a salt and pepper beard and matching head of hair, looking at them and making a motion with his hand for them to put their window down.

Micah looked at Cassie who was staring blankly at him before he pushed the button to make the window disappear into the door.

"Hi. Looks like you must be lost. No one ends up here if they could help it," said the man laughing, his blue eyes sparkling.

Cassie and Micah looked at each other, not sure how to respond.

"I'm just kidding. The name is Jeremiah Ashtor. My friends call me Jerry. Where were you headin'?" he asked taking a blue handkerchief out of his jeans pocket to wipe away the sweat that gathered on his brow.

"Well, we want to go to Lakewood Amusement Park, but we keep getting lost. Even our GPS can't get us there," responded Micah.

Jerry chuckled again. "I don't trust those things myself. Give me an old-fashioned map."

Cassie sat up straighter in her seat. She was starting to like Jerry more and more.

Just as Cassie was going to say she agreed with him, there was a slam from the front porch.

"Jerry, are you bugging those poor people?" said a medium statured woman, a little on the hefty side in her yellow flowered printed dress. She wore her blondish-gray hair in a messy top knot and pushed her dark-framed glasses onto her nose before placing her hands on her hips.

"I was just going to tell them how to get to the amusement park, dear. (She is so nosy.)," he said just quiet enough to be heard by Micah and Cassie. "Then I'm going to send them on their way."

"Oh no you won't," said the woman coming off the porch and walking toward them. "They have to stay for dinner at least. You can't travel anymore on an empty stomach."

Just as Micah was going to protest, the woman talked over top of him. "No. I won't take no for an answer. I have some chicken, homemade mashed potatoes, green beans, homemade bread and butter, and chocolate cake. Doesn't that sound good?"

Before Micah could answer, Jerry was already opening their car door.

"Best just to listen to her. Take it from me, she always gets her way."

"That's right," she said while playfully hitting his stomach with the back of her hand.

Feeling like they didn't have much of a choice, Cassie and Micah got out of the car.

"See. Was that hard?" She looked at the two of them. "I'm Bess, but everyone calls me Momma B. What are your names?"

Micah and Cassie introduced themselves as they stood in the gravel driveway.

"Come on in. Dinner is almost ready. Our son Danny will be here soon, and then we can eat. Also, I have something you two might like inside," said Bess leading the two up the creaking steps and into the house through the front door.

Once inside, Jerry shut the door behind them.

"Just this way," said Momma B going into a room to the left of them.

Cassie and Micah followed with Jerry tagging along.

Once they were inside, Cassie and Micah couldn't believe what they saw.

All around the room were glass cabinets and shelves holding all types of memorabilia connected to "Carly's Nightmare."

There were movie posters, first edition signed copies of the book, original scripts, and more.

"I thought you would like it," said Momma B, as proud as a peacock. "Jerry will give you a tour as I finish dinner. Make yourselves at home."

Micah and Cassie couldn't believe their luck. They had found a true fan of the book and movie while on their pilgrimage.

Jerry led the two around and explained how he had worked as a construction assistant on the film and that's how he got everything.

Just as he was showing them the set design for the carousel, a voice said from the door frame, "Never thought I would see you two again."

Micah and Cassie turned to see who was talking behind them.

Leaning against the door frame with his shoulder and his arms crossed and feet intersecting at the ankles, was the guy from the store where they had stopped to ask for directions

"Name's Danny. Sorry if I made you uncomfortable earlier. I didn't mean to. We just don't get a lot of visitors," he said taking off his "Steve" hat while nervously playing with it in his hands. It seemed like he genuinely felt bad about creeping them out earlier.

"No worries, man," said Micah giving it a shrug.

Danny looked across the room at Cassie. His eyes traveled all over her. She crossed her arms over her chest and turned her attention to another artifact from the production of the movie.

Momma B came into the room and told the group dinner was ready and to follow her into the dining room.

Despite the creepiness of Danny, Micah and Cassie liked Jerry and Momma B. They were nice people that wanted to offer whatever meager means they had.

Once in the dining room, Momma B said they should be seated at one of the light oak chairs that were placed around a large table made of the same material.

After they settled, Cassie looked around the room and saw a matching China cabinet full of blue and white plates and bowls that looked like they were heirlooms.

Adorning the walls was a stuffed deer head on one side and a bear head on the other.

These types of trophies always made Cassie uncomfortable. They reminded her of her uncle's house, the same uncle that she had a less than stellar relationship with.

She felt a shiver down her arms, but quickly shook it off as Momma B walked into the room carrying a huge plate of fried chicken that she sat in the middle of the table.

She then ducked back into the kitchen like a busy worker bee. This time she came out with a bowl full of mashed potatoes in one hand and the other had buttered green beans.

Momma B sat down the bowl of green beans and went around the table and put heaping spoonful of mashed potatoes on everyone's plate. She followed this with the green beans, bread, and butter before she poured everyone a tall, frosty glass of lemonade.

"Dig in," she said as she took her seat opposite of Jerry as the heads of the table.

Micah and Cassie could hardly wait. They had been so hungry from all their traveling. They hadn't eaten much that day except for a banana and some mixed nuts at the airport.

The mashed potatoes melted in their mouths and the meatloaf was seasoned just right with the perfect amount of gravy on top.

One bite of the delicious food made Micah and Cassie relax a little. The food served as a way to revive them from all the time spent in the car.

The conversation was lively and went back and forth about the film industry, Micah and Cassie's home, and even about the town of Seraphim Falls.

After the last of the food was eaten, to the point where Micah and Cassie felt like they were going to pop, Momma B left again and produced a chocolate cake.

Micah and Cassie said they couldn't eat another thing and they needed to get back on the road. But Momma B said she wouldn't take no for an answer and set down two huge slabs of dark, chocolate cake in front of them.

It did look good to Micah and Cassie, so they figured they could have a little dessert before getting back on the road to find a hotel for the evening.

After dessert was over, Micah and Cassie got up to leave. Micah was talking to Jerry about directions to a nearby hotel while Momma B was packaging a few pieces of cake for the road.

Even Danny said if they needed any type of oil or stuff for their car they could stop by and he would give them a good discount.

Micah and Cassie got in their car and drove away waving out the window.

Following Jerry's directions, Micah arrived at a small motel, fifteen minutes away.

He turned off the car and went in to see if there were any vacancies.

After a few minutes, he returned with a key to room number seven.

He pulled the car over to a parking spot right outside the door.

"I got a map inside that should take us right to the park tomorrow," he said passing over the map to his girlfriend.

They both grabbed the few pieces of luggage they had and dragged them into the small motel room.

It seemed clean and worn at the same time.

Micah flopped down on one of the double beds with a bounce. It was covered with a sickly green comforter that looked straight out of the 1970s. Even the blue shag carpet looked like it was lifted from the same decade.

"It doesn't seem to be too bad. A little firm, but good for one night."

Cassie smiled and went over and laid down next to him, nestling into the crook of his arm.

"I'm just happy we seem to be headed in the right direction," she said.

Micah didn't give a response. She looked over at him. His chest was gently rising and falling,

She picked up her head to get a better look at him. Suddenly she began to feel shaky, and beads of sweat began to form on her arms. The room started to pick up and swirl around her.

Cassie reached over and grabbed Micah by his forearm and shook him gently at first and harder when he didn't respond.

"Micah." was all she could croak out before the room went black and Cassie's strength left her.

Micah woke up. His head was pounding like he had a terrible hangover.

When he opened his eyes, everything was blurry and there was a hazy, darkness floating through his eyes. Micah reached up to rub them away but found he couldn't move his arms or his hands.

He shook his head in an effort to gain his sight back. It worked a little and he could see he was in a dimly lit room. The walls looked like they were made of dirt and the ground crumbled away when he dug his feet into it.

Micah looked around and didn't see much except for a kerosene lamp on a crate and a few dirty blankets.

Fear started to creep into his throat and his lungs began to feel constricted.

Being that he suffered from panic attacks regularly, Micah did his breathing exercises and was able to clear his head a little.

"Cassie," he whispered not wanting to let his captives know he had awakened.

He whispered louder this time, no answer.

Micah began to panic not knowing what happened to his girlfriend.

He looked around the room and noticed a sharp and slender rock was near his right foot.

Micah reached out and put his foot on top of it. Just as he was getting ready to drag it back to him, he heard a noise above him. It sounded like heavy footsteps. After a few moments, the noise stopped, and a creak replaced it as light flooded into the room down by Micah's feet.

Two feet appeared on the top of the step. They were dark brown, working boots that stepped heavily down the steps followed by a pair of blue jeans, a blue and white checked shirt, and finally a salt and a peppered beard and matching shaggy hair.

"Good to see you again, Micah. We are so glad to have you come and visit us so soon," he said.

"What am I doing here? Where's Cassie?" he yelled at the man that was getting closer and closer toward him.

Jerry bent down and stared at Micah. There was nothing behind his cold, blue eyes that seemed so warm and friendly yesterday.

He said nothing as he continued to stare as a smile drew across his face. It wasn't welcoming, and it wasn't friendly, but Micah couldn't put his finger on what emotion Jerry was giving off.

"You will see her soon. But, right now, let's have some 'man time.'"

Jerry reached behind his back and pulled out a knife. It glinted in the little amount of light that was radiating from the kerosene lamp only a few feet away.

He held the knife close to Micah's face so that he could see that Jerry meant business.

Jerry took the knife and slowly reached around behind Micah.

Micah closed his eyes and squinted, preparing himself for the amount of pain that would follow Jerry plunging the knife into his flesh. But he was surprised when he felt the tension around his arms loosen and the ropes fall away.

Micah brought his arms to the front of him and rubbed his sore wrists that were rubbed red and raw.

Jerry let out a big belly laugh and threw his head back.

"I wasn't going to kill you, boy. You need to learn to relax."

Micah looked at him like he wasn't sure how to respond to Jerry.

Jerry re-sheathed the knife behind his back and grabbed Micah by the arms and lifted him to his feet.

"Up you go," he said placing him, upright, on the ground. "I want you walk up these steps. But I don't want you to get the idea to run," he said to Micah, his face close to his. "If you take off, I will have to kill you."

Micah swallowed hard and gave a quick nod to Jerry. He couldn't see any other choice.

He climbed the dirty, wooden stairs slowly. His legs were wobbly and felt heavy as he plunked down his feet.

Micah had to shut his eyes once he emerged from the underground bunker. When his sight had finally adjusted, he could see he was in the room where Jerry kept all of his movie memorabilia.

He turned to see Jerry slam a door in the floor and roll a rug over it to keep it hidden.

Jerry looked at him and smiled.

"You didn't know what you were standing on earlier, did ya?"

Micah began to feel sick in his stomach. The meatloaf, mashed potatoes, green beans, and cake were churning. He could feel it starting to come back up his throat, but he swallowed hard to keep it down.

"Let's have a talk in the kitchen," Jerry said to him while grabbing him by the arm and guiding Micah through a door straight ahead.

Once they were in the next room, Jerry sat Micah down at the table. It was a smaller version of the dining room table with the same light wood, but it only had four chairs.

Micah looked around and could see the typical kitchen with a refrigerator, stove, microwave, and medium-toned wood-colored cabinets in front of blue wallpaper that had lighter blue stripes running vertically.

Before Jerry or Micah could say anything, another door that was to the left of the one they had gone through, swung open. In walked Momma B carrying a large metal bin full of ground meat.

"Hello, sweetie," she said looking at Micah and walking across the room to put down the heavy load.

The white apron that she wore over the same dress Micah saw on her earlier was covered in blood. It looked like she had been butchering meat in the basement. No doubt it was some wild game if the deer and bear heads in the dining room were any indication.

"We were just going to have a talk," said Jerry to his wife.

"Don't mind me. I'm going to just package this stuff for the freezer. Pretend I'm not even here."

Momma B went to work busily putting the meat into pre-made plastic bags and sucked the air out of them with a machine.

"Listen, Momma B and I was talking earlier about you and Cassie. We saw how hungry you were and how thin the two of you seemed. We want you to stay a little longer so we can help you put some weight on."

Micah looked at the man sitting at the table across from him and went slack jawed. He looked at Momma B who was still busy packaging the meat.

"Let me get this straight. You are holding me here against my will because Cassie and I are too thin, and you are worried about our health?"

Jerry kept his face stone and turned toward Momma B who had stopped what she was doing and turned to look at Jerry.

Micah jumped as they both laughed loudly like that was the most ridiculous thing someone could have said.

Once they composed themselves, Jerry turned back to Micah and said, "We don't care about your health. We want you and Cassie to fatten up. Because right now, you would taste terrible."

Micah could feel the blood drain from his face and the room melt away from him. His head was beginning to spin. He thought Jerry was joking but looking at the seriousness of his face and seeing all the meat Momma B was packaging he knew it wasn't a joke.

Right at that moment, the door that leads to the dining room slammed open and in walked Danny, dragging Cassie by the arm. He shoved her roughly into a chair.

"I brought her in for ya', Maw and Pa," he said backing and leaning against the counter.

Momma B walked over to Danny and gave him a hug. "You are such a good boy for helping us."

She gave him a gentle pat on the cheek and then went back to work.

Micah tried to reach out to Cassie to comfort her, but Jerry put a stop to that by separating them on opposite sides of the table.

"It's sweet and all, but we can't have that happening," he said moving Cassie while scraping the chair on the floor causing a loud screech.

Micah looked over at Danny who was staring at the floor. He was obviously upset about something.

Jerry noticed too and said, "What's wrong, Danny-Boy."

Danny continued to play with a piece of string that he found in his pocket.

"Why do I always have to be here for this part," he said.

"Because everyone does their fair share," responded Jerry.

"But why can't I be like Curtis or Mikey. They don't have to do the dirty work."

Jerry rose out of his chair and walked across the room to stand in front of his son. Micah and Cassie could see how much smaller Danny looked next to his father. It was like he was still a child in the eyes of his family.

"Curtis is the salesman of the family and good at renting the cars, and Mikey has the technical know-how. You are the brawn."

Micah wasn't sure he had heard right what Jerry was saying to his son.

"Wait a minute. You mean Curtis from the rental car company is your son?" he asked, his voice going up an octave. "The same Curtis that we rented our car from?"

"That's my boy," said Momma B beaming with pride. "Isn't he a charmer?"

"Then who is Mikey," asked Cassie who was also afraid of this answer.

"This is where it gets really good," said Jerry taking his seat back at the table. "You see, we need a steady stream of fresh meat. We can't eat our neighbors, because people would notice 'em missing. So, we need to find people who are just traveling through. We didn't want to have to dispose of their vehicles after we processed them, so our idea was to go after people who need rental cars. This way the car goes back to the rental place, and no one is the wiser."

Micah and Cassie turned toward the stove as they heard a sizzle and saw Momma B was frying up patties of some of the meat, she had previously been packaging.

"Here is the best part. We had to find a way to make sure these people would end up at our house. So, Curtis would ask people where they were going to visit while they were in the area, and then he would tell our other son Mikey, the tech wiz, and he would program the rental car's GPS system to always lead 'em to our house. No matter what address they put in. People are so trusting of technology, so it was always easy."

Micah and Cassie looked at each other. Micah felt guilt wash all over him. If he would have just listened to Cassie about the map they wouldn't be in this predicament.

"And if people still weren't trusting the GPS, there was always Danny at the store who could lead 'em to us with his directions," said Jerry. "We thought of it all."

Jerry leaned back in his chair looking triumphant. Danny looked around the room and seemed nervous. Every so often Micah could see him look at Cassie and then get a pained expression on his face.

Micah knew he had to find a way to get him and Cassie out of this situation. It was his fault after all.

Just as he was thinking of a solution, a plate was plunked down in front of him. On it were two cheeseburgers.

"Eat up," said Momma B. "You won't find any cheeseburgers better than these."

"She's right. The last batch we had were already fat enough, we were able to butcher them right away."

Both Jerry and Momma B laughed again, while Danny looked disgusted.

"Lighten up, Danny sweetie. After all, you did get that nice shirt and hat out of the deal."

Danny looked like he wanted to crawl out of his skin. Jerry saw this and grew red in the face.

"You got a problem, boy, with this family," Jerry rose from his seat again and walked over to his son. "We put up with the fact that you are a vegetarian, but I will be damned, if you look down on your kin like that ever again. If you keep it up, we will make you into burgers. Understand, me?"

Danny nodded slightly while still staring at the floor before looking over at Cassie.

"Ohhhhh, I get it now," said Jerry in a mocking tone. "Hey Ma, our boy has a little crush."

Momma B turned to look at her son as Jerry went over to where Cassie was sitting, He grabbed her by the head and held it in place.

"Let her go," yelled Micah.

Jerry ignored him.

"You think she is pretty don't you. Do you honestly think she would be interested in you? Look at you. You are nothing but a backwater, redneck, who is dumber than a brick. What do you have to offer her? Just watch as she recoils when you look at her. Tell me I'm wrong."

Jerry released Cassie's head. She started to cry.

Momma B rushed to her side. "Don't cry, darling. It isn't that bad. We won't let Danny hurt you."

"I said let her go," yelled Micah standing up.

"If you know what is good for you, you'd sit back down," said Jerry from across the table.

"Like hell, I am, old man," he replied, with his eyes looking dead into the eyes of Jerry.

Without breaking eye contact, Jerry rose from the table and walked over to Cassie. He grabbed her by the wrist and pulled out the knife he kept sheathed to his belt.

"If you don't sit down and eat that food in front of you, I swear to all that is holy I will chop off her fingers," he said holding the knife over her pinky.

Micah looked back at him. He didn't want Cassie to get hurt, and he couldn't tell if Jerry was bluffing. He stood there for what seemed like only a few seconds before Jerry said, "I warned you" and brought down the knife on Cassie's right pinky finger, severing it from above the second knuckle.

Cassie howled as pain seared through her body. Blood ran out onto the table in time with her heartbeat. In only a matter of seconds a quarter of the table was covered in crimson.

"Damn it, Jerry. Don't make a mess in my kitchen," said Momma B turning around to find a dish towel to bandage Cassie's finger.

In a split-second while Momma B's back was turned and Jerry was looking at her, Danny leapt across the room and tackled Jerry.

The two fought on the floor of the kitchen. Danny was on top trying to get the knife away from his father while Jerry was writhing around in efforts to get his son off of him.

Momma B screamed and threw the towel on the table toward Cassie and tried to pull her son off of her husband.

Cassie grabbed the towel and wrapped it around her finger. The blood was still flowing causing the cloth to look like roses blooming through the winter snow.

She looked around the room until she found what she wanted. Cassie stood up, reached behind her to grab the frying pan full of hot grease. She picked it up and smacked Momma B in the back of the head.

The woman howled as grease went down her back scalding the flesh on its way. She turned to look at her attacker. Then Cassie hit her again square in her forehead, but this time she dropped to the floor.

Jerry was distracted for a brief second at seeing his wife crumple to the floor.

Danny used this to his advantage and was able to grab the knife from his father and plunge it deep into his left side.

Jerry yelled in pain as the knife stayed firmly implanted.

Danny got up and rushed to Cassie's side.

"Look. I know you could never have feelings for me as I do for you, but I couldn't stand the thought of you becoming like all of my parents' other victims. Just promise me that you will live a happy life and never come back here. I don't think my heart could bear it," said Danny as he held on to Cassie's shoulders.

Cassie stood there frozen for a moment.

"Micah, get her out of here before it's too late," he said turning to him.

Cassie leaned in and gave Danny a kiss on the check.

She saw a smile stretch across his face with sheer joy, then it morphed into a frown before he dropped to the floor next to his mother. His white shirt started to turn pink then a deep red color.

Cassie panicked. She didn't know what had happened until she saw Jerry rising behind him holding his bleeding side with one hand and the knife with the other.

"I always knew the boy was too soft."

He used his foot to kick his son, who was bleeding out on the ground, out of the way so he could get closer to Cassie and Micah who was now by her side.

"I don't like to harvest this soon, but you give me no choice."

Just as Jerry was lunging toward the couple, one of the kitchen chairs slid in front of Jerry causing him to trip, and stumble to the ground.

Micah and Cassie looked down and saw Danny's hand holding the chair's leg.

"Run," he croaked out before his body went limp for the last time.

Cassie grabbed Micah by the hand and pulled him out the front door, down the porch, and toward a beat-up, blue pickup truck.

They tried the door handles and were able to open the door and get inside. Both Micah and Cassie slammed down the buttons to lock the doors. Micah searched everyone inside the truck for the keys. Luckily, a pair were concealed in the driver's side visor.

Both Micah and Cassie prayed as he put the keys in the ignition. This was their only hope of escaping this nightmare. When the truck roared to life, Cassie and Micah exhaled a little.

Micah pushed the start button, as they both prayed the car would start. When it did, they breathed a sigh of relief.

Micah put the truck in reverse, just as they heard a noise like a buzz go by their heads. They looked out the front of the car and saw Momma B standing on the front porch with a shotgun. Her face was deep blue and purple where Cassie had hit her with the pan and blood had matted a section of her hair.

"You come back here and eat the food I made you," she yelled just as she was lining up her next shot.

"Go to hell," Micah said as he punched the gas and reversed out of the driveway.

Another shot rang out into the clearing, this time it hit the passenger side mirror, but Micah kept going until he could put the car in drive and turn around.

He sped away from the house back down the winding road they had followed earlier.

When they passed the convenience store, Cassie felt sadness wash over her. She wasn't sure what she felt about Danny, but she couldn't ignore the fact, he had put his life in harm's way for her. It hadn't been Micah.

Micah and Cassie drove away in silence, through the town of Seraphim Falls, and back on to an interstate that led them to an uncertain future.

# Laugh in the Dark

iz stood in front of the mirror and adjusted her shirt. She loved the way the hunter green polo looked against her dark skin and how it coordinated with the navy-blue shorts. Sure, they looked like "mom shorts," but she didn't mind it. How was she supposed to do her job if her shorts were riding up all day?

"Now to put on the finishing touch," she said.

Liz threaded her thick, wavy hair through the back of a green baseball hat with the words "Lakewood Amusement Park" stitched on the front.

While most eighteen-year-olds dreaded having a summer job, Liz couldn't wait. It was a welcome change after the events of last summer; something she preferred to not think about.

A buzzing come from her phone that was right next to her on the nightstand in her bedroom. She reached over and saw she had a text from her friend Olivia.

*Olivia: Ready to join the rest of us working stiffs?*

Liz smiled. Olivia had been working each summer for the past four years at a mom-and-pop dinner called "The Moose Tail." She hated the job, hated the lousy tips she received from customers, and hated smelling like fried food at the end of her shift. But Olivia desperately needed to have the money so she could start college in the fall. It was no secret that after Olivia's father lost his job as a coal miner four years ago, money had been tight for her family.

Liz's situation was a little different. Her parents had recently divorced, but her mother's lucrative job as the vice president of the town's chemical company made sure she would have no problem attending college. Liz was working to get some extra income to help with everyday expenses that would pop up while she was at school.

*Liz: Can't wait! I got the uniform on and I'm ready to go.*

*Olivia: I have to see a pic. Txt me after work.*

"Liz! You have to leave if you don't want to be late for your first day on the job," yelled her mother from downstairs.

"I'm coming," she replied.

Liz ran a brush one last time through her ponytail that was cascading down her back, in between her shoulder blades.

She grabbed her purse and raced down the steps where her mother was waiting for her.

"You look great, Honey!" said her mom.

She reached out and encircled her daughter in a hug.

"I can remember when I worked at Lakewood when I was your age. It was a wonderful experience and I had so much fun."

"And the money for college doesn't hurt, too," said Liz.

She looked down and rummaged through her denim hobo bag that she had slung over one shoulder.

"I told you not to worry about the money. You have a lot of scholarships that will take care of most of the expense, and your father and I will help with the rest," said her mom.

She reached out and cupped her daughter's chin so she could bring her attention back to her.

"Just enjoy one of your last carefree summers. You don't have many more left before you spend your time working."

Silence hung between them. The topic of summer always left a pall in the room when Liz was involved.

She shrugged it off as her hand emerged, victorious, with her car keys.

"I gotta go. I'll be home after my shift," she said.

"Do you have everything you need," asked her mom?

"Yes, Mom. I never go anywhere without it now."

Her mother smiled and drew her in for one last, big hug before Liz turned and walked down the front porch toward her bright yellow, 1970 VW Bug she had named "Fernando." Even though he was a little cantankerous at times, Liz loved the car and had so many great memories with it.

She opened the door to her car and tossed a book from her driver's seat over to the passenger's seat. It was about the expressionist Edvard Munch. His famous painting "The Scream" was on the cover.

"Yeah, me and you both, buddy," she said talking to the book.

Liz backed out slowly from the driveway and waved to her mom as she put the car in drive and rambled down the road.

It was only a quick ten-minute drive along twisting and winding back-country roads before Liz was pulling into the employee's parking area at Lakewood Amusement Park.

She turned off Fernando, grabbed her purse and stepped out of the car. Liz couldn't believe she was going to work at a place where she spent a lot of her time growing up.

Liz spent so many summers with her parents going to the park when she was little and then going with her friends when she got older. Her first ride on a roller coaster was here. She could remember how much of a "big girl" she felt when she took her first ride on the "Lil Tiger." Sure, it was a baby coaster, but it was a big deal to her. The way her Dad held her tight as they went over the little hills, and the way she laughed with his arm around her, was one of her most cherished memories.

As she walked toward the employee entrance, Liz reached into the bottom of her purse, found her ID badge, and clipped it to the collar of her polo shirt.

"Good Morning, Miss. Heading in for your first day," asked a guard that was working the gate?

"I am," she said.

The older man who looked to be in his mid-fifties was a little overweight and had tufts of gray hair sticking out from under his uniform cap.

"The name is Don, and we will be seeing a lot of each other," he said.

A smile drew across his face, and Liz could tell she was going to like Don.

"If you need anything, just give a holler."

She handed Don her employee badge. He looked at her smiling picture and matched it to the face that was in front of him. Then he gave it back to her.

Liz smiled and nodded as he pressed a button that activated the security gate to open and allow her inside.

She paused for a moment and turned toward Don.

"I'm supposed to meet a Daryl Carr. Do you know where I can find him?"

Don chuckled, his full belly jiggling like Santa Claus.

"Don't worry, he will find you. Just head toward the back of the park."

Liz wasn't sure what Don meant, and she wasn't a fan of surprises.

She didn't want to be late, so Liz decided to follow Don's directions.

The gate closed behind her and Liz had her first taste of the park when it was empty of guests.

It was eerily quiet. Liz was used to hearing lots of laughter and gleeful screams from the attractions. But to be left with her own thoughts and occasional tweets from birds left her on edge.

Since she knew the layout of the park like the back of her hand, navigating to the area that Don had mentioned was easy.

She passed the silent carousel, saw the "Brain Fryer" steel coaster lying in wait for its first round of thrilled riders.

Sweet smells of cotton candy and deep fryers were starting to waft in the air indicating the day's food preparations were already underway.

When she reached the back section of the park, which was home to attractions like the bumper cars, The Whip, and the iconic Ferris Wheel, Liz didn't see anyone around.

"This is where Don said to go," she said to herself.

She looked around for anyone, but no one was in sight.

Liz walked over to the bumper cars.

"Hello," she said, as her voice echoed in the pavilion. No answer.

Her tennis shoes crunched over the gravel as she walked to the Ferris Wheel. She looked all the way to the top but couldn't see anyone.

She went to The Whip, and it was the same story.

There was one attraction left that she hadn't looked at yet, and she was dreading even going near the place.

Situated in the very back of the park, away from attractions that were too afraid to be near it, was "Laff in the Dark."

Ever since she was little, Liz hated this ride. The large face, on the outside of the building, with the giant grin missing a few teeth scared her. The automated laugh that was blasted from the speakers near the attraction made her cover her ears.

Each year her friends begged her to go on it, even trying to drag her to the entrance of the dark ride, but Liz always dug in her heels and refused to get any closer.

Liz said a silent prayer hoping this wasn't going to be where she was working. She closed her eyes really tight and repeated under her breath, "Please don't let this be it. Please don't let this be it."

"I'm sorry to disappoint you, but this is it," said a voice behind her causing her to jump a little.

Liz whirled around and saw a man standing there.

He looked like he was in his late forties and had dark, wispy hair that was combed over the top to hide the ever-widening bald spot. Silver glasses with oversized frames, that look like they belonged in the 1980s, rested on a rounded nose over a neatly trimmed beard.

The man wore the same shirt and dark blue shorts Liz had on, but they hung like soaking wet laundry on his small, wiry frame.

Liz glanced over to the right side of his chest and saw a name tag that read "Daryl."

"Sorry to scare you like that, you must be Liz," he said extending his hand. "I'm Daryl, your supervisor for the summer."

Liz shook his hand and smiled back. Her first impression was she liked Daryl, even though he scared her just a moment ago.

"I hope you aren't afraid of the dark because this summer you are going to be stationed at this beauty," he said.

Daryl gave a grand sweeping motion with his hands before placing them on his hips and staring at the building with a smile on his face. Liz wasn't sure but she almost felt he was looking at the attraction lovingly.

Liz's stomach began to churn.

*This would be my luck, to be stationed at the worst attraction in the whole park for the entire summer.*

She didn't have the heart, or even want to tell Daryl her true feelings about Laff in the Dark. It would make her seem like such a problem on the first day.

The words of her therapist flashed in her head.

*Try and do something each day that makes you a little scared. It can help you grow, and it might be the key to getting you to overcome your obstacles.*

"Nope. I'm all good." Liz lied through her teeth. Daryl's smile grew even wider on his face. It was almost as big as the toothsome grin that made Liz feel uneasy.

"Great! Let me show you around!"

Daryl waved his hand toward Liz, wanting her to follow behind him.

He walked around the side of the building, pulled out a key ring from his pocket, and unlocked a side door.

"This is where we keep our personal items, look at the schedule for the day, and grab the paperwork for our maintenance reports, he said." "You can store your bag here."

Daryl held the door open for Liz to grab the paperwork and to stash her bag before he squeezed past her into the tight space.

He then went over the inner workings of how safety checks were conducted, how Liz would be scheduled, etc.

"Now that we have that boring stuff out of the way, let's get to the good stuff. Follow me."

Daryl flashed his big smile and winked at Liz. He led her out of the room, locked the door behind him and walked around the back of the building; the place where guests were never allowed. For Liz, it felt like the curtain was being pulled back and she could see "The Wizard" that was pushing the buttons and pulling the levers.

Daryl reached a maintenance door, unlocked it with the same keyring, and groped around in the darkness until he found a light switch.

Lights blinked on near the inside of the door as if the building was waking up from a long night of sleep. Daryl ducked inside.

Liz stood frozen for a moment just outside the door. Sure, the lights were on just inside, but as she looked past the entrance, she noticed everything else was pitch black except for a few small areas that had dim emergency lights.

*This is ridiculous, Liz. You can do this. It is just a stupid ride. How bad could it be?*

Liz psyched herself up mentally, took a deep breath, and followed Daryl into the back of Laff in the Dark.

She looked down and couldn't see even her hands in front of her face. She carefully shuffled her feet along the floor in hopes of bumping into something before tripping over it. She could see a light ahead as she made her way to Daryl, accident free.

"I thought maybe I lost you there," said Daryl, half-joking while also being serious. "Are you okay with working here? If not, I could request a change for you ..."

Before he could finish his sentence, Liz interrupted, "Nope. I'm fine. Just first day jitters."

*He'll never believe you. You are such a terrible liar.*

Daryl looked at her, trying to get a read if she really was okay or not.

He decided to shrug it off and continued his spiel.

Liz looked around the room with the only available light coming from Daryl's lantern.

Daryl saw her looking and walked over to the wall and flipped a switch. Suddenly the room was flooded with light and all of the dastardly props were exposed to be rubber masks and Halloween decorations on hydraulics.

She saw spooky paintings on the walls of witches boiling body parts in a big cauldron, and the devil dancing around in flames with a pitchfork in hand. They were overly cheesy.

Basic animatronic, nothing more, nothing less. The smell of mechanical oil gave away the mystery that surrounded how things worked here.

Liz could feel herself relax. She even began to appreciate the attraction for what it really was: a goofy attraction created to give people a harmless jump scares to make them feel silly afterward.

"The biggest thing you have to worry about in here is people getting 'too close,' if you know what I mean," said Daryl with a wink. "We each take a turn watching the security cameras. If it seems like things are getting inappropriate, radio me and I will take care of it. T rarely happens, but it still occurs on occasion."

Liz covered her mouth so Daryl couldn't see her smile. She had heard from her friends at school what would typically go on in here.

"But that's all you really need to know. Do you have any questions?"

Liz thought for a moment but realized Daryl had given a very thorough tour and she couldn't think of anything.

She shook her head, and Daryl said if she thought of any to just ask away.

He looked down at his watch and said, "It's almost time for the staff meeting. We better head to the main pavilion. There you'll meet Jack, who is the other crew member on Laff."

Liz walked with Daryl and the two talked about the upcoming season at the park and all the excitement surrounding "Sahara," a new steel coaster debuting later in the summer.

Once they arrived at the main pavilion, a covered picnic area in the heart of Lakewood next to the lake, Liz saw there must have been a hundred employees gathered. She had no idea the park employed that many people.

Daryl led her over the grass that was still slightly damp from all the humidity the day before and toward a picnic table. Sitting there as if almost waiting for them was a guy with tanned skin, sandy brown hair that dusted the tops of his ears, and a killer smile.

"This is Jack. Jack this is Liz, she is going to be on the Laff team with us this year," said Daryl.

Jack reached out his hand for Liz to shake. When she gripped his palm, she could tell just by the handshake that he was a confident guy, and he knew that opportunities would just open for him. But, when she looked at his eyes, she could tell there was kindness behind them.

"Nice to meet you, Liz. Welcome aboard. It isn't a bad gig once you get past working with Daryl," he said. "I've been working with him for about two years now and I've just started to like him."

Daryl shot him a look in return that showed an understanding that Jack was just gently ribbing him. Liz felt that maybe it wouldn't be so bad working the attraction this summer. At least she liked her teammates.

As she took her seat between Daryl and Jack, she looked around at all of the other employees that she would be spending the summer with. A lot of them were just like her, college kids or those getting ready to go to college in the fall. There were some older people, like Daryl, but they were probably in management positions.

"Are you in high school or college," Jack asked?

"I just graduated this spring. I'm going to Willamette University in the fall."

Jack leaned back in his chair and whistled. "Willamette? That's pretty prestigious. You must be very smart."

Liz could feel her face growing warm. She didn't know how to respond without sounding like she was bragging. She knew she was smart but didn't like people to think she was TOO smart. Then they would start to make assumptions that she is a snob, or all she does is study.

This wasn't true about her at all. But part of her also used this as a shield to prevent people from knowing her real truth. Something she had to keep hidden at all costs.

Jack must have sensed Liz's apprehension because he continued.

"I'm in my second year at State. It isn't bad; good party scene and the classes aren't killer."

Just as Jack was going to ask Liz another question, the PA system kicked on with a screech.

"I guess this is on," said the voice. "Welcome everyone to our first staff meeting of the summer season."

Liz looked out over the sea of about 200 people and spotted a taller woman with brown hair cut into a pixie cut holding a microphone near her mouth. A smile beamed across her face as the applause erupted over the excitement about the upcoming season.

As the noise died down, she continued.

"Thank you for the warm welcome. As you know this summer is going to be another great season for the park. But, before we talk about all the exciting things we have planned for this year, we do need to discuss a few items."

The woman looked down at the clipboard she was holding in her hand. Liz guessed it held her notes to help her remember everything she wanted to discuss at the meeting

"For those of you who don't know, I'm Hannah Pizzeria, and I'm the general manager of Lakewood Amusement Park. I look forward to getting to know these new faces I see out here and catching up with those of you who I have worked with before."

Liz could tell that she was going to like this woman. The fact that she was wearing the same shapeless uniform as the rest of them meant she wasn't afraid to get down on their level. Liz felt this is a key factor in a good boss.

"While a lot of exciting things are going to be taking place, there is one unpleasant topic I need to address first.

"Many of you know one of our own, Jonas Emmerson, has gone missing. His family has been holding out hope and continuing to search for their son and brother, but so far nothing has been discovered. The police are still continuing their investigation. So, if you have any information about his disappearance or his whereabouts, please contact me or the Seraphim Falls Police Department. Any information, no matter how small you think it is, can make a big difference."

There was a slight pause as Hannah let the appropriate amount of time pass before she talked about something more pleasant.

"This year also marks the fiftieth anniversary of the park. In honor of this momentous occasion, we are going to have a special evening on July 28, where we will close the park to guests and invite all employees, past and present, to enjoy an evening in the parks for free, including a delicious dinner buffet."

Again, thunderous applause rose from the crowd. Everyone was excited to have the day to enjoy the park and to reconnect with some of the friends they have made in the past

Hannah continued to go over more housekeeping information and announced "Sahara" would officially open on July 1.

"If anyone has questions, please stop by and see me or ask your team captain. With that, let's get in our places to open the gates."

Everyone cheered and slowly ambled to their stations for the day.

Liz, Jack, and Daryl walked back to Laff in the Dark to prepare it for the day.

"Since this is your first day, Jack why don't' you show Liz how to load people onto the ride where all the security monitors are."

A look of slight apprehension crossed Liz's face before she could hide it.

"It's actually pretty easy. You just make sure there are no more than two people in the front and two people in the back. Double-check their lap bar is pulled down and locked in place, and then off they go."

Daryl opened the door to the loading area of the attraction before he walked over to a dull, metal panel.

"If there is a need to stop the attraction, walk over to this panel here and press the red button. I have confidence you can handle it."

Jack, who was standing next to Liz, flashed one of his signatures, bright smiles and gently shouldered her.

Daryl went to go to the security room and left the pair to stand in front of the line for the attraction.

Slowly, Laff in the Dark began to come alive. The old woman began her haunted laughs out front, the spooky soundtrack began to loop, and Liz could hear and smell the oil from the hydraulics kicking in as they began to spring to life.

After only a few moments, a group of guests began to queue up.

Jack took the first group of four, disbursed them among the two rows, told them to pull down their lap bars, and checked to see they were locked in place. Then with a whirl and a groan, they disappeared through the swinging doors that were painted to look like the mouth of a giant skull.

"See! It's easy. Now it's your turn."

Liz did the same thing Jack did with her group of four. Everything went off without a hitch.

"You've got it! You're a natural. Also, make sure they get off the attraction. You can keep an eye behind you when they come back through the two double doors. If anyone is having a hard time getting out, come over to the panel I showed you earlier and hit the red button. It will slow the attraction to a stop giving the guests more time to get out of the vehicle."

Liz nodded her understanding.

Everything was going smoothly for the first two hours. Liz was loading people into the cars, Jack was positioned at the panel watching the cars enter the haunted house, and Daryl was in the security room keeping an eye on everything.

Two hours after park opening, Jack got a call over the radio.

"Jack. I need you to suspend the ride for a moment. There is an issue with Mr. Bojangles. Send Liz in. I want to show her how we fix the damn things. Over."

Liz heard everything Daryl said over the radio.

"Copy," he said before putting the radio back in his pocket.

Jack reached down and hit the stop button and picked up the mouthpiece on the intercom.

"Everyone please remained seated while the ride is at a stop. We are experiencing some technical difficulties and expect to have everything up and running in a few short moments. Please remained seated."

Jack let go of the button and re-attached the mouthpiece to the panel.

"You need to find Daryl. He'll show you what to do. This happens a lot," said Jack.

Liz nodded. She was fine working the front area where she wasn't actually in the attraction, but having to go inside now, made her stomach start to churn.

She walked to the side of the building, unsure about the situation. She pulled the flashlight from her pocket and started to think of all the horrible things that could pop out at her when she was inside.

When she reached the service door, Liz knocked a few times and Daryl swung it open toward her.

"I wanted to show you what to do in case this happens, which is all the time."

Daryl sighed heavily and shook his head in disgust.

"You think with all the money they rake in each summer; they could put a little back into the attraction."

Liz walked inside and switched on her flashlight as Daryl closed the door behind her.

Liz couldn't see much of the attraction. Her flashlight provided very little illumination.

She was able to spot Daryl moving in front of her. She figured if she kept the beam of light straight in front of her, focusing on the back of Daryl she would end up where she needed to go.

Liz kept her focus on the hunter green polo shirt in front of her until it stopped moving.

"This is Mr. Bojangles. He is constantly breaking down," said Daryl pointing his flashlight at a large white skeleton that was outlined with neon green paint that would glow when the black lights were turned on.

Liz could hear a type of grinding noise. It was as if Mr. Bojangles wanted to break free but was being held back by something. For a moment, Liz couldn't believe she was able to personally identify with this overgrown, Halloween decoration.

Daryl took an oil can he had in his hand and squirted the black, shiny liquid onto the bottom hinge of the animatronic. When he was happy with the amount of oil dispensed, he put the can down, took a cloth and rubbed the dark, sticky, liquid into the base.

"Now, he should be all good," he said taking a step back to admire his work.

Daryl then pressed a button at the base of the machine, and it sprung to life, giving Liz a start.

The way its face twisted when it launched forward to scare the passersby made her feel uneasy.

Daryl chuckled. I didn't mean to scare you."

Liz shrugged it off. "It's okay. I just wasn't expecting it."

Daryl grabbed his radio and switched it on. "Go ahead and fire it up. Everything should be working now."

From the other end of the walkie-talkie Liz could hear Jack say, "over" and the attraction whirled to life.

Daryl motioned for Liz to follow him out of the attraction. She had to duck a few rubber bats suspended from the ceiling with fishing line and watched so she didn't trip over a black cat howling and hissing from the floor.

When they got nearer the exit, Liz looked over toward the left. There was a door there Liz hadn't seen before when she was on the tour Daryl had given her.

Instead of being framed by cinder blocks like the rest of doorways in the attraction, this one looked like it had a heavy, dark frame. Liz couldn't see for sure in the darkness, but she thought there were carvings surrounding the frame.

She tried to shine her flashlight over toward the new opening, but each time she did, her beam of light would cut out. Like there was a short in the flashlight. It seemed like the door was trying to keep its secrets hidden.

Liz wasn't sure what was propelling her, but she crept closer toward the door as the sounds of the attraction whirled around her. Her feet crunched on loose pieces of dirt and gravel and the smell of gasoline and ride grease was starting to make her head swim. One foot in front of the other as she went closer to the newly discovered doorway.

*I have to see what is over there. If I could just get a quick peek.*

Suddenly, Liz felt something grab her arm and yank her backward, just as a black, heavy object flew over her head.

"What are you crazy?! You are going to get yourself killed," yelled Daryl over the hum of the machinery while he dragged her back toward the service opening of the attraction and into the blinding sunlight.

"What the hell did you think you were doing?" asked Daryl as he bent over, hands on his knees, panting like he had run a marathon. "I had to yank you back or else you would be part of the attraction as the headless ghost girl."

Liz began to feel shaky. She wasn't sure what had come over her. One minute she watching Daryl apply oil to the base of an animatronic and the next thing she was being yanked outside after almost being killed.

"I'm sorry," she stammered. "It won't happen again."

Daryl's face softened as he looked at Liz, the nervous teenager standing in front of him.

"It's alright. Just never forget where you are. Just because you are in a fun house, doesn't mean it can't be dangerous"

Liz nodded in understanding.

"What were you looking at anyway?"

Liz tried to gather her thoughts.

"I'm not sure. But there was a door to the left of the one we came out of. It was different than the other entrances. This one was surrounded by wood and had what I could guess were words, carved into it. I was trying to get a better look."

Daryl smiled and laughed a little, "I guess the fumes got to you, huh?"

Liz screwed up her face in confusion and crossed her arms over her chest not liking the feeling she was having. "What do you mean?"

"There are two doors in that place. The one we went in and out of and one that leads to the security room. There is no doorway with wood framing."

Liz began to feel hot all of a sudden. It was like Daryl's words were being said at the end of a very long, narrow tunnel. She began to sway a little on her feet.

Daryl noticed and said, "Why don't you take your first fifteen-minute break. Get some air and a bottle of water. It will do you some good. When you come back, you can take the next security shift, okay?"

Liz nodded. The idea of getting away from Laff in the Dark seemed like a good one.

She left and waved at Jack as she walked toward the center of the park, and away from the attraction.

All employees were given tickets to get bottles of water throughout the day as well as a meal for either their lunch or dinner break.

Liz decided to stop at Sammy's Seafood on a Stick Shack to get her water.

When she got there, she immediately regretted the decision as the smell of fry grease and seafood made her stomach do flip-flops; she hated the smell.

She handed her water ticket to a guy named Marcus. Quickly, he returned with her water and she decided to walk to a nearby bench for her break.

The park wasn't overly crowded considering it was opening day. The threat of an afternoon thunderstorm probably kept a lot of people away, not wanting to pay the exorbitant ticket price for only a half-day of fun.

Liz looked at her watch and saw her fifteen minutes were almost up. She knocked back the rest of her water and threw it away in a garbage can right next to the bench.

Just as she was starting to stand up, a person sat down next to her.

"It's a great day at the park, isn't it?" said a boy about her age wearing the same type of polo shirt and shorts as she was, but his shirt was red, and the shorts were khaki colored.

"It really is. I hope the storm passes us by, though," she said looking at herself in the reflection of his aviator sunglasses. Liz noticed his shaggy, brown hair was like Jack's, but it was longer and went to almost his shoulders.

"You never can tell how things are going to turn out around here," he said turning his face away to observe the guests getting their food at the seafood shack.

Liz was able to get a better look and noticed his name tag read "Simon".

"Have you worked here long," she asked?

Simon gave a little chuckle. "For a while. Sometimes it seems like I never leave."

Liz smiled and nodded. "I hear sometimes in the middle of the season the work hours can be long and brutal."

Simon broke his gaze from a woman in a sunflower printed dress buying a soda from the shack.

He turned to face Liz and took off his glasses so he could stare at her more intensely. There was something about his deep emerald eyes that made Liz feel uneasy.

"You don't know how brutal it can be," he said, his voice dropped lower and was barely above a whisper. "Don't' go where the light won't go."

Liz began to feel sweat forming on her palms. The back of her neck was soaked under her thick, curly ponytail, and her mouth ran dry.

"What do you mean?" she asked him, her voice shaking.

"You know what I mean. You were lucky today. Don't let it happen again."

His voice sounded breathier like the words were trying to slither out of his mouth. Liz couldn't pinpoint it, but this made her feel uneasy; like she wanted to find a place that was safe to hide.

"Uh. Okay. Thanks. See you around," she said.

Liz stood up from the bench, not breaking eye contact with him as she began to walk away, a little unsteady on her feet. She knew she had to get out of there as fast as she could. She wasn't sure what Simon had tried to tell her, but she didn't like the way it made her feel.

Her feet felt like lead and her knees tried to buckle as she walked away from him. Once she was about fifty feet away, she turned to look back at the bench and saw he was gone. Liz wasn't sure if his sudden disappearance was a relief or did, she now feel more concerned.

She wound her way through the groups of laughing and smiling people, who she was sure wasn't having to deal with creeps and weirdos like she was.

When Liz reached Laff in the Dark, Jack was standing in front of the ride loading people into cars.

"Hey Liz, how was your break?" he asked over his shoulder while pushing down the bar on a young teenage couple who looked a little over-excited for rubber skeletons and black light paintings. No doubt they were more interested in the "dark" part of the attraction.

"It was fine," she said hurriedly. "I have to get back and do security, but I wanted to ask you something first. Do you know a guy named Simon who works here? A little weird, brown shaggy hair, wears red polo and tan shorts?"

Jack stopped for a second and looked like he was searching his mind for the person that would match the description.

"Doesn't ring a bell, but he could be one of the coaster guys. They never hang out with the rest of us, they think they are better than everyone else," he said while starting to help a mother and younger child, who looked terrified, into their seats.

"You might want to ask Daryl. He has been around here for longer than I have. He might know."

Liz nodded and turned to leave to take her post. She didn't want to be late after her first break. Especially after she almost killed herself in the attraction.

She turned the knob and walked into the closet area that served as the headquarters for Laff in the Dark's security.

Seated on a folding chair, in front of six small black and white monitors, was Daryl.

Liz's eyes moved from Daryl over to the wall where a large poster of Edvard Munch's "The Scream" was hanging.

Daryl looked at Liz and noticed what she was staring at.

"Yeah. I thought it might brighten the place up a little. Plus, considering where we work, I thought it might be funny."

Daryl then mimicked the signature open mouth scream from the painting and a laughed a little.

Liz stood there looking at him, not sure what to say. The painting had both intrigued and made her feel uncomfortable.

Daryl noticed the look on Liz's face. He dropped his hands and cleared his throat.

"Feeling better," he asked?

Liz noticed he didn't take his eyes off the screen when he talked to her.

"Much. Just needed a little water," she said.

Liz leaned against the back wall. The coolness of it felt good on her back that was dripping with mid-day sweat.

"Good to hear. I need a break myself after looking at these screens for so long," he said standing up from the chair so Liz could sit down. "All you do is make sure no one is doing something that would hurt themselves or get the park in trouble, you know what I mean?"

Liz nodded.

"If you see something, radio Jack first, he will shut down the ride, then radio me and I'll go take care of it. Got it?"

"Yep. Can do," she said.

Liz's eyes cascaded over the black-and-white monitors, trying to get her bearings on the attraction.

On the first one, she could see the young child and mother Jack was loading into the car when she was talking to him. The poor kid had his eyes screwed shut and clung to his mom for dear life.

"Before you go, Daryl, I have a quick question."

"Shoot," he replied.

"Do you know a guy named Simon who works here? Shaggy brown hair that goes down his neck, a little bit of a creepy vibe, wears a red polo and khaki shorts?

Daryl thought for a moment, the same way Jack had when Liz asked him.

"That's odd you should mention that. There was a guy named Simon Jasper who had worked here. He was a coaster guy, a little odd, but harmless. But that was few years ago. It was the middle of the summer season and he just stopped showing up for work. People called him and tried to find out where he was, but no one could get in touch with him. Hannah even went to the address he had listed on his emergency contact form. His parents answered the door, they told her to never come back to their house, and then slammed the door in her face. It was so strange."

Daryl started to stroke his scruffy beard as he thought back to that time.

"Not sure who you could have been talking to, but it wouldn't be a current employee. Everyone wears the same uniform colors that we have. The red and khaki uniforms that you were talking about changed about four or five years ago.

Daryl pushed off the wall with his back and gently patted Liz on the shoulder.

"Anyway, have fun. This is my favorite part of the job. People try some strange things in there," he said.

When Daryl left, Liz sat in silence for a moment. *What had I seen? Who did I talk to?*

Liz mulled over the questions as she finished the rest of her shift that seemed to pass quickly. She could see what Daryl had meant about being on security duty for the attraction was his favorite position. She was able to sit, in air-conditioning, and just keep an eye on the monitors. Luckily, nothing happened during her shift.

Later, Daryl came and told her she was all done for the day and that she is going to be a great asset to the team. Liz started to feel more comfortable being at Laff in the Dark. She liked Daryl and Jack and really felt like she fit in with them.

That night, during dinner, Liz and her mom talked about their experiences working at Lakewood. They laughed at how little changed in more than 20 years.

"I can't wait to go to the reunion picnic," said her mom.

Liz smiled as her mom came over to get the plates from the table and take them into the kitchen.

An idea popped into her head.

"Mom, did you know a coaster guy named Simon when you worked there?"

Her mom stopped in the doorway between the kitchen and the dining room.

"The name doesn't seem familiar, but then I didn't hang out with the coaster guys. They kept to themselves. They looked down on those of us who didn't operate 'thrill rides,' and believe me, no one was going to confuse the carousel with a thrill ride."

Her mom turned away laughing softly to herself while she took the dishes to the kitchen, thinking of a memory.

Liz helped clear off the rest of the table before she went upstairs to her room. She shut the door behind her and sat down at her desk. She touched the mouse and the screen on her computer sprung to life.

She typed a search engine into the address bar and then did a search for "Simon Jasper."

The first item that came up on the search appeared to be a news article.

Liz clicked on it. When it loaded, she let out a large gasp.

In the 2015 article about the disappearance of Simon Jasper, a 17-year-old employee of Lakewood Amusement Park, was a photo of the same kid she had talked to on the bench earlier.

Her throat started to tighten and breathing became harder.

*Practice what Dr. Preachman had taught you. Count to four, hold for four, and then breathe out for eight.*

Liz used the breathing technique she had learned from her doctor last summer. It almost always worked, but this time it seemed to only make things worse.

Liz shut off her monitor and went into her bathroom. She opened her medicine cabinet and scanned the shelves for the right bottle. She grabbed the amber colored vessel and took out one pill. She filled a glass with water from the sink and slugged it, along with the pill, back.

In a few moments, Liz could feel the tightness loosening from around her chest and the panic seemed to leave her. She hated taking the medication, but at times like this, it was needed.

Feeling better, and more tired, Liz crawled into her bed and feel into a deep, dream-less, sleep.

The next month seemed to pass by quickly at Lakewood. Liz had settled into a groove and really enjoyed her working days. The only cloud that seemed to constantly hang over the amusement park was the occasional detective that was still investigating the disappearance of Jonas. Liz was interviewed by an officer but didn't have much to say because all of this happened before she started working there. Olivia came and visited her at work a few times. Liz had an idea it wasn't as much to see her but, to check out Jack.

Liz couldn't believe how quickly the summer was flying by, and before she knew it, it was time for the employee reunion.

You couldn't have asked for a better day, weather wise. It was sunny and in the mid-eighties.

Liz was gathering her beach bag so she could shove extra sunscreen, her sun hat and sunglasses inside.

"Come on, Liz, we don't want to be late," her mom yelled from downstairs.

She took one last look around the room to make sure she had everything she needed and then left the room, closing the door behind her.

Her mom was standing at the bottom of the steps wearing jean shorts and a khaki-colored polo shirt that had Lakewood stitched over the right breast.

"So, how do I look?" her mom asked turning around as Liz reached the bottom of the steps.

Liz couldn't help but smile. She knew her mom was looking forward to the picnic today and couldn't wait to catch up with old friends. Her energy was almost infectious.

"You look great, Mom," said Liz smiling. It was so nice seeing her mother truly happy, considering everything that happened last summer.

"We are going to have a great time today. I can't wait for you meet some of the old crew," she said reaching out and grabbing her sunglasses to put on top of her head.

Liz and her mom walked out of the front door and into the car to begin the drive toward the amusement park. When they got there, Liz's mom had to show her invitation and Liz had to show her employee badge since only those who were invited to the special event could get into the park today.

Liz's mom parked the car and they walked toward the entrance. At the front gate they were handed a schedule of the day's events. Glancing over everything, Liz saw that she is supposed to work a shift and then a former employee would be coming by to relieve her before everyone would gather for lunch in the picnic grove.

Liz's mom promised to swing by "Laff" with her friends while Liz was working and then they could go to the picnic together.

Liz bounded off toward the back of the park and could feel the excitement of the place pulsing through her. On her way, she passed several excited groups greeting each other with hugs and happy shrieks. It seemed like Lakewood was a special place for a lot of people.

When she reached "Laff in the Dark," Liz saw Jack standing out front and Daryl was talking to someone off to the side.

"Excited crowd today," said Jack as he leaned against one of the attraction's support structures.

"It seems that way," said Liz as she put her hands in her pockets. "A lot of people in the community grew up coming here and when they were old enough worked here. It's like an institution or a way of life."

Jack looked out into the crowd. It seemed like there was something bothering him.

Liz was going to ask if everything was alright when Daryl walked over and interrupted.

"Okay, Laff crew, today is a special day as I'm sure you know. We will have different crew members in and out all day. We take the first shift and then an alumni crew will come and relieve us."

Liz and Jack nodded their understanding.

"Liz why don't you take security, Jack you do loading, and I'll do some crowd control."

Everyone agreed and understood their positions and took off in their directions.

Liz opened the door to the small security room and was meet with a rush of cold air. It seemed like the AC was working overtime today. The office that was always a little chilly seemed frigid today.

Liz shook it off and sat down in the metal folding chair before she flicked all of the security monitors to life. The black and white picture wobbled a little before it snapped in place and gave a clear view of what was going on inside the attraction.

She was surprised at how many people were already starting to board the attraction.

"It must bring back a lot of fond memories," she thought as she watched a couple in the 50s get "a little cozy" in their car as it roared to life through the doors of the attraction.

For twenty minutes Liz watched car after car pass through the double doors that looked like a woman's buck teeth and emerge into the other side of the darkness.

Her eyelids started to get heavy, and she had to fight the sleep that was threatening to take hold of her.

When Liz caught herself actually sleeping, she opened her eyes and saw something that she didn't expect to see on the middle monitor: it was that strange door again. The door with the wooden frame and the carvings. The same door that Daryl told her didn't exist.

She blinked hard and took a drink of water before returning her attention back to the screen.

But there it was. Standing almost proud and boastful defying anyone to try and tell it didn't exist.

Liz watched as cars went past it and no one paid attention to it.

She leaned in closer, feeling the warm static of the monitor on her face. She thought she heard something. She held her breath so she could listen better.

That's when she heard it over the beating of her heart in her ears. It started off quiet but grew louder and louder.

It was laughter.

It wasn't the laughter of a young child, or people who were feeling a wave of adrenaline after experiencing jump scare, but the laughter that came from deep down inside. The kind that starts as a low rumble, like a thunderstorm in the distance, and then crawls out of the mouth like a wave of emotion.

It didn't seem sinister, but its intent wasn't joyful either.

Liz didn't know what to do. She couldn't call for Jack to stop the ride. What would she say, "Jack, stop the ride, I don't like how someone is laughing?" It would make her sound even crazier than she already felt she was.

*I have to make this go away. It's just my imagination.*

Liz thought for a moment, and then came up with a solution.

She reached into her pocket and took out a small, blue, plastic container. It was about the size of a silver dollar and screwed apart. Inside were two small, white pills.

Dr. Preachman had told her they were only for emergencies, only for when things got beyond her control. She felt seeing doors appear out of nowhere and hearing phantom laughter was out of her control.

She put one of the pills on her tongue and swallowed hard.

Liz felt the medication glide down her throat and knew in about fifteen minutes she would feel a lot better. She would be more in control. That was one thing she learned last summer. She could handle almost anything as long as she felt she was in control.

She sat back in the folding chair and continued her job of watching the monitors. She could feel the panic that was caught in her throat start to sink back down, and she felt like she could breathe again.

Liz began to fall back into the ease and comfort of the job when the door flew open and in walked Jack.

"My turn to sit in the AC," he said walking into the room. "You get to sweat it out in the heat and deal with the guests."

Liz laughed. "Fair is fair," she said getting up from her seat. "Don't work too hard."

"I never do," Jack said smiling as he sat down on the folding chair.

Liz shut the door behind her and walked to the loading platform as her handset buzzed.

"I forgot to tell you Daryl is taking a break. He ran into some chick he used to have the hots for back in the day and they left to get a soda. So, you will have to go and deal with any pain in the asses on the attraction," Jack said over the speaker.

"Roger. Over and out," she said back to him as the gravel crunched under her feet.

The thought of Daryl hitting on a woman made her almost laugh. She had no idea what his pick-up lines would be considering he spent most of his time working on a comic book with his brother or serving as dungeon master for his D&D group.

Liz squeezed past the guests waiting in line and went to the front to start helping load people into the cars. Everyone was nice and accommodating and nothing major had happened.

It was such a nice day and Liz was really enjoying herself and spending time with the guests. A lot of people recognized her because she looks so much like her mom, and they would share memories of her mom.

Just as she was helping to belt in a woman who was one of the original ride operators of "Laff," Liz got a buzz on her walkie.

"Hey, Liz. I need you to shut down the ride. There is a kid in there trying to hang out of the car and grab on to the animatronic. He is right by Mr. Bojangles. Can you go in and talk to him?" came Jack's voice over the speaker she had in her hand.

Liz groaned before she pushed the button to talk back.

"Roger and over," she said before holstering the walkie at her hip.

She walked over to the panel and pressed the red button to make the attraction stop. She then made the announcement over the speaker to tell everyone to please remain seated.

Liz grabbed her flashlight and walked through the swinging double doors of the attraction.

Once inside she clicked on her light and jumped when the portrait of a man with flesh melting off his skeleton greeted her.

Even though she has been in lots of times before, she still is caught off guard by all of the props and special effects.

"Damn thing," she said under her breath.

*Pull it together, Liz. You have been in here lots of times before. It's no big deal.*

Liz was able to calm herself and turned to the right to follow the track into the haunted cemetery scene. She knew the kid that she was looking for would be around the corner only a few feet ahead.

The problem was Liz had a difficult time finding her way around. A thick fog had descended on the area and clouded her vision. It was a struggle to see where the beam of her flashlight ended. The fog machine sometimes fritzes out and would overproduce the fog causing some guests to even choke on it.

She reached down to her side and grabbed her walkie.

"Jack, can you turn off the fog machine. This is getting ridiculous. I can't see anything. I think it's having problems again," she said pressing the button on the walkie in her hand.

There was silence.

Liz waited for a minute before reaching out to him again. All the while the fog was getting heavier and heavier.

"Jack. Seriously. It's getting hard to breathe now."

Once again silence hung in the air almost as thick as the fog before a response came buzzing over the flimsy connection between the two walkie talkies.

"You don't like to listen to people, do you Liz?" said the voice on the other end.

The hair on Liz's arms stood on end. That wasn't Jack's voice. She wasn't sure who it was, but it sounded familiar. Her head started to buzz because of the fog and because of this strange voice that was communicating with her.

"Who the hell are you?" she asked trying to make herself sound braver than she was. Her voice only shook a little as she tried to practice her breathing exercises to calm her.

*Four breaths in. Hold for four. Eight breaths out.*

"I tried to tell you. I tried to help you, but you wouldn't listen. Now there is nothing I can do," the voice hissed above a whisper at the end of the walkie-talkie.

Liz held the neck of her shirt over her mouth to try and help filter some of the fog so she could breathe.

That is when it clicked in place for her.

"Simon!" she yelled. There was no response. The fog continued to cloud her.

"Simon!" she yelled again. But the line was dead.

Liz knew she had to get out of there as soon as possible. She felt she was in danger but wasn't sure exactly what she was in danger from. She put her hands in front of her and shuffled her feet making sure not to trip over the track. She had to evacuate all the guests from the attraction too.

As she walked, Liz's hands bumped into a cold smooth surface. She reached over the top and could feel the sticky vinyl of the ride's car seat.

"I need you to calmly unbuckle your seatbelt and exit the vehicle. You will need to grab onto my shoulder, and I'll get you out of here."

There was no answer or movement. Liz thought this was strange because she had personally loaded each ride vehicle and she knew they were all filled.

Liz shuffled her feet toward where the next car was. Again, there was no one inside. She wondered if maybe Jack had helped evacuate people.

Liz's breaths were getting more and more shallow and knew she had to get out now. While trying to make her way to the exit, her hands would occasionally grope a Styrofoam tombstone or the edge of a wooden crypt. It wasn't much, but it was enough to guide her to the next area. After working for a few weeks, she knew the interior layout pretty well.

Once she exited the cemetery scene, the fog had disappeared. She found it strange that it would just go away like that, but she was happy she could breathe again. She leaned over, with her hands on her knees, and took several deep breaths. Welcoming the rush of air into her depleted lungs.

When her breathing was back to normal, Liz stood up to her normal height and shone her flashlight around the room.

There was Mr. Bojangles in mid-spring waiting for his next victim and right next to it was a ride vehicle, frozen in place.

Liz could feel anger start to bubble to the surface.

*If this stupid kid could just behave, I wouldn't have to be in here right now.*

She walked up to the vehicle trying to calm herself so she wouldn't get in trouble for yelling at a patron.

"Excuse me. You have to stop touching the attraction or else you will be kicked out," she said walking up to the waiting ride vehicle.

Once she reached the purple and gray wagon that was supposed to look like a hearse, she saw no one was inside.

Liz remembers how she thought Jack had evacuated everyone because of the fog.

Something popped into Liz's head and she began to get angry at first, but then decided to laugh it off.

"Ha. Ha. Very funny, guys. You did get me good," she said over the walkie talkie. "I especially liked the warning and the whole 'Simon' thing. So, who is he, Daryl, someone you used to work with many summers ago?"

There was silence yet again.

"Guys," said Liz, the tightness returning to her chest. "This isn't funny anymore. Answer me."

As if right on cue, a low rumble started in the corner of the room and radiated toward her in the form of a laugh. It was the same laugh she had heard over the monitors earlier.

Liz shone her flashlight over the darkened corner, but her light went out before it got to the area. Just like before.

In the darkness, Liz squinted and could only make out the same mysterious frame with carved words from before.

"Alright, Liz. Let's face our fears. Like the doctor told you, 'fears hold you back and keep you stuck,' and I'm feeling pretty stuck."

Liz squared her shoulders and edged toward the doorway.

The laughter continued, like a beacon guiding her toward a safe place.

After twenty feet, Liz reached the frame. She ran her fingers over the smooth, cold surface. Every so often she would feel an indent carved into the wood.

Her fingers searched the words trying to read what was etched before her. But everything was written in a type of language she didn't know.

A feeling deep inside her stomach radiated from her bellybutton and began to propel her forward. She had no choice but to continue walking straight through the door that Jack hadn't seen, and Daryl had assured her didn't exist.

The compulsion took over and she crossed the entrance of the frame and into darkness.

The air seemed thick and smelled stagnate, like time had stopped and everything on this side had decided to hold its breath. Liz could do nothing but stand inside of the swallowed darkness.

"You just couldn't stay away," said a voice that sounded a lot like Simon's, but also seemed different at the same time.

"But, since you are here now, welcome home."

# The Hotel Arcadia

Her brown hair whirled around like a halo of soft curls as she roared down the highway in her powered blue, 1966 Mustang.

It was the car she always dreamed of having and now it was finally hers.

Tucked in the backseat was her tan, hard-shell suitcase, packed to the point of explosion with belongings that she couldn't live without.

But the most significant thing she brought along with her was her sense of freedom.

Now, she could do anything she pleased, with no one telling her how to live. Not her boyfriend, not her mother, not even society.

*Maybe I will finally get that cheeky little flower tattoo I've always wanted,* she thought to herself as she sped down the road, kicking up dust behind the wheels of her tires.

She drove on for what seemed like hours before she noticed the sky starting to darken over the surrounding desert.

The dusty road that stretched out before her started to seem menacing instead of the pathway to freedom it had appeared to be just a few minutes ago. She had never liked the dark and hated storms even more.

Wanting to reach a hotel before it turned to night, she looked around at the passing road signs that indicated what exits had lodging.

*After all, you can't set off on adventure if you are too tired.*

The landscape continued to disappear behind her, while in front of her the sun started to settle giving a spectacular light show of pinks, oranges, and purples before dipping below the horizon.

She passed a billboard on the right side of the road advertising The Hotel Arcadia. The picture boasted a lavish boutique resort with rich reds and warm golds done in the Art Deco style. She thought about it for a while, whether she should keep going until she reached Las Vegas, or if it would be better to rest for the night. She went back and forth for a while, as the Arcadia hung in her mind.

With her decision made, she turned her wheel sharply to the right and took exit 52, just like the sign had told her to.

The woman continued to follow more signs advertising the hotel until she reached a grand driveway. She was relieved to finally be at her destination because the darkness had finally settled in.

One thing that wasn't difficult to see was the large building with red awnings over the front windows situated at the end of the long driveway. The building's dark, gray brick was awash with light from several spotlights that illuminated the front of the building. The lush landscaping of well-trimmed boxwoods and rhododendrons was the icing on this already impressive cake.

Her car purred to a stop as she pulled to the entrance and gazed inside to see the interior had matched what the billboard had promoted.

She turned the car off, grabbed the suitcase from the backseat, and walked through the doors.

The heels of her black shoes clicked over the ebony, white, and gold tiled floor consisting of diamond geometric patterns. Large, red velvet chairs were staggered throughout the lobby in various sitting areas and around black, glass coffee tables with gold edging.

As her fingers inched through the brown curls, in hopes of taming the unruly mass, the woman looked to the right and saw the hotel bar and a similar color scheme.

A real-to-scale tree was in the middle of the bar. It wasn't like an ordinary tree. Gold metal branches twisted and entwined with each other as golden leaves perched on the ends. Underneath of some of the leaves were what the woman thought were apples. They were the size of the fruit, but they looked like they were giant rubies hanging, waiting to tempt someone.

She shook her head thinking the precious metal arbor was overkill. A little on the tacky side for her taste, but then again, this hotel was a little more opulent than what she was used to.

She looked to the left and saw glass doors leading to what appeared to be an indoor swimming pool. The crystal waters were reflecting the various marble statues standing sentry at the edge of the aquatic area. It reminded her of a picture of a Roman Bath she once saw in a book when she was younger.

She continued past the dark red drapes cascading from the ceiling and ending in a crimson pool on the floor. Eventually she reached the front desk that was made of the same black glass and gold trim.

She looked around and couldn't see anyone working behind the counter. She tried to peer into the doorway behind the desk, but the same heavy, red curtains obscured her view.

Realizing the baggage, she was carrying was starting to get heavy, she looked at the floor and set it down at her feet. When she brought her eyes back up to the counter, she gasped.

"I'm sorry to startle you, ma'am," said a tall, slender man standing behind the front desk.

"It's alright," she said trying to compose herself. "I would like a room for the night. My name is …"

Before she could finish, the man with the long, dark hair slicked back into a braid running down his back, put his hand up to stop her from speaking. She noticed his hands were full of wrinkled mountains and valleys; a trait that didn't match the man's youthful complexion that was looking back at her.

"I know who you are already, but here, we don't use real names," he said lowering his hand and busying himself finding a paper behind the desk.

While he set about this task, the woman had an opportunity to get a better look at him.

He was tall and thin, but she could tell under his red velvet jacket and black button-down shirt, he was more muscular than gaunt.

His nose and lower half of his face came to a point that reminded her of a bird. A type of bird that was more into blood and bone than seeds and berries. The way he was looking around on his desk was reminiscent of being in the middle of a hunt, narrowing down on the kill.

He moved around gracefully like a dancer and carried himself with an air that indicated he held all of the secrets of this place. The aura around him made it seem like his job, maybe even his life, depended on keeping these secrets.

"Here it is," he said interrupting the woman's thoughts. "Ms. Monet, I need you to sign here on the dotted line."

He extended a pen to her, and she took it while looking at him quizzically.

"Why the need to change my name?" she asked while signing the artist's name on the line.

"It just makes things easier."

He took the pen and paper from her, filed it away in a cabinet and then turned around, placing both hands on the desk in front of him.

"This is The Hotel Arcadia and I'm Raphael. If you should need anything, day or night, I'm here for you. What makes us unique is our hotel is split into two very different sections that each offer a unique experience. Tonight, you will choose between either the East or West Wing. You have three days to decide to stay where you are or try out the other wing. At the end of those three days, you will be assigned your living quarters for the remainder of the time you are with us."

The woman began to become confused.

"But I'm only here for tonight," she tried to tell Raphael, but he didn't pay any attention, he went on with his spiel.

"Each side has its own benefits and shortcomings. You decide what you can and can't live without. Do we understand each other, Ms. Monet?"

The way he peered at her, she felt even more like a rabbit under the peregrines gaze.

"Yes," was all she could squeak out. She didn't understand the rules totally but felt she would figure them out sooner or later. Anyway, what kind of hotel has rules on where you could stay? This seemed absurd, but if she wanted a place for the night, she should just go with it, for now.

"What will it be ma'am; the East or the West?" he asked first extending his arm to her left, toward the pool, and then his other arm to her right, toward the bar.

Monet looked around the room. How was she supposed to make a decision just based on a few hallways and the lobby of the hotel?

"Which would you choose?" she asked the man behind the desk.

A wide grin drew across his face. It was a smile that Monet didn't much care for. It made her uneasy in ways she couldn't describe.

"That is a decision for you to make. It isn't up to me."

She let out a huff, "Fine. I'll take the East Wing."

"As you wish, Ms. Monet," he said bowing his head toward her. "I'll have a bellman take your bags to your room."

He turned around and produced a key from the board that was hanging behind him.

"You will be in room 28. It's just up the stairs, the fourth door on the right."

Raphael paused for a moment, as if interrupting himself.

"I tell you what, how about I make you a deal, we love deals here at The Hotel Arcadia," he said grinning at her again. "I'll also give you a key to the West Wing. You can check it out, see if you like it. If you want to switch, let me know and I'll change your arrangements immediately."

He extended his hand with both keys. Monet took them quickly. She wanted to get out of this man's gaze as quickly as possible.

"Have a wonderful evening," he called after her as she walked away from him and toward the center of the lobby.

She didn't get very far before he called out to her again.

"Oh, just to let you know, I wouldn't leave your room after one a.m.," he said.

Monet turned to look at him.

"Why is that?"

That same grin that had spread across his face was back now.

"Just trust me," he said before he turned and disappeared back between the velvet curtains.

Monet stood, rooted in her position, as she tried to shake away the uneasiness Raphael left her with. She slipped the keys into the purse, that she just noticed she was gripping onto for dear life causing the blood to drain from her knuckles and wasn't sure what she wanted to do next.

"That was a tough decision, wasn't it," said a male voice that was obscured by the opulent piece of furniture.

Monet walked around one of the velvet chairs and saw a man sitting there. He was medium build, looked to be in his late 30s, and wore a neatly trimmed beard. His jeans and plaid work shirt seemed out of place in such a lush setting.

"It was. What were we supposed to use to make our decision?" she asked taking a seat in the chair across from him.

"At least we have a few days to change our minds," he said, picking at an invisible spot on his jeans.

He brought his brown eyes up to meet hers and reached over to extend his hand," The name's … well, I guess I shouldn't give you my real name for some stupid-ass reason. So, my name is Picasso."

Monet reached over and shook his hand and introduced herself using her artist's name as well.

"This is a strange place alright," she said gazing around the room.

"Tell me about it. I am pretty sure I was the only one staying in the East Wing until you came along," he said.

"What made you choose East," Monet asked.

"I don't know. It was just the first thing that came to mind when he asked."

Monet played with the tassel hanging from her purse.

"Did you have a chance to go over and check out what the West had to offer," she asked?

Picasso paused for a moment, lowered his eyes and played with a rouge thread hanging from the tail of his shirt. "Never bothered. Just figured it's okay where I'm at so why look for anything else."

"If you ask me, West is best," came a voice from over at the bar.

Monet and Picasso stood up and saw a young woman sitting at one of the stools to the left of the tree.

"Why don't the two of you come join me instead of standing there staring," she said, holding her cocktail in the air.

Monet and Picasso looked at each other, before walking through the rest of the lobby and up the few steps that lead to the extravagant bar.

The two took a seat on either side of the woman who had long, dark flowing curls tucked behind her ears that were studded with pearl earrings. Her black dress plunged deeply and was highlighted by a matching pearl necklace. She looked like a femme fatal out of a 1940s gangster film.

"I'm Kahlo," she said looking at her two new companions. "Monet and Picasso, right?" she said looking at them using their assigned names.

They nodded in agreement.

"Barkeep, bring my new friends some drinks. Put it on my tab," she said waving her hand over her head with a flourish that seemed to giveaway that this wasn't her first drink of the evening.

A man, who wore the same type of jacket and shirt as Raphael, came behind the bar from a room to the left.

"I'll have a glass of Pinot Noir," said Monet.

"Miller Light for me," said Picasso.

Without a word, the barkeep found the requested bottle of beer and set it in front of Picasso with a glass and poured Monet the wine she requested.

He then turned and left without saying a single word.

"Friendly fellow isn't he," said Monet as the sweet and slightly bitter wine tantalized her. The same rush of adrenaline she used to get from drinking came back to her. It had been a few years since she kept her promise of giving up the vice that had controlled her life. But, since she was starting her new life, what could it hurt.

Kahlo's words brought her back to the present.

"I kind of like the strong silent type," she said with a wink.

"So where are you two heading?" asked Kahlo as she took another long swing from her cocktail that smelled like a mixture of cherry juice and gasoline.

"I'm going to Las Vegas," said Monet. "I've always dreamed of going there, but there was always something or someone holding me back. Now, for the first time in my life I finally feel free."

"Ah! Sin City! I like that," said Kahlo with a wink. "What about you, cowboy?"

Picasso looked at Kahlo. He wasn't sure how he felt about being called cowboy, but because she was so damn attractive, he didn't really mind it.

"I'm on my way to Texas to buy a ranch. I've always dreamed of owning one, and I woke up one morning and thought, what the hell."

Kahlo nodded her approval.

"I'm in the same boat. I'm on my way to Hollywood to try my hand at being an actress," she said with a flourish that made Monet think she would be perfect for one of those overly dramatic soap operas.

"Just like you Monet, I felt held back. Trapped really since I was a kid. I was always living in my sister's Shadow and I had no way of escaping."

Monet and Picasso nodded politely at what Kahlo had shared. A silence hung in the air until Monet changed the subject.

"It seems like we are all here as a brief stopover for something greater," said Monet before she sipped her wine.

The Pinot slipped down her throat so easy and so smooth. She was worried she was going to pay for it in the morning.

"Amen, Sister," said Kahlo lofting her glass in the air. "So, you two are Easters, huh?"

"Yep. Not sure what to base the choice on when I first arrived, but I figured having the pool on my side of the building would be nice. The room is nice and comfortable, and I couldn't see what more I could want so that's where I am," said Picasso.

"How about you, Monet," asked Kahlo?

"Same. Sort of. When I looked at the pool versus when I looked over here, the pool made me feel more comfortable. My heart felt lighter, if that make sense. So that is why I chose it."

"You should at least check out your West Wing option. You don't know what you are missing," Kahlo said.

"Why did you pick the West," asked Picasso?

Kahlo finished her drink in one long gulp.

"I, like the two of you, originally picked the East Wing. It was okay but wasn't exciting. I wanted to see what was over here. So, I took a trip after my first night. When I opened the door to the West room, I couldn't believe my eyes. There was everything I could have possibly wanted, clothes, jewelry, high-end makeup and more. If I had all this, I would for sure land an acting job."

Monet and Picasso couldn't believe what Kahlo was saying. Monet felt it was too good to be true, and Picasso didn't have a need for such extravagances.

"Well, I think I'm going to go to bed now. I hope to get going in the morning. Wish me luck."

And with a wave of her hand and well wishes from her drinking companions, Kahlo left and was off to the West Wing.

Monet and Picasso finished their beverages and stood up to leave the bar.

"Walk you to your wing," he asked?

"Sure," said Monet.

The two walked through the lobby toward their hotel rooms.

"I don't know about you, but it just doesn't feel right to get all that stuff," said Picasso talking about what Kahlo was saying about her room in the West Wing.

Monet nodded in agreement.

"Look, I have made some mistakes in the past, some big ones. I didn't help people when I should have, and I let people get hurt when I could have done something about it," said Picasso suddenly getting sad. "There was this one time I did help someone, a woman. It changed my life. I don't remember a lot about it, but I think it was my undoing. But I'm okay with that. I still feel like I have a lot to make up for and I feel a fresh start is the best way to do this."

The duo walked the last bit in silence. It wasn't an uncomfortable silence, but more of an understanding. Picasso felt better telling someone about his past, and Monet was happy to feel she wasn't alone.

When they arrived at the door to the first-floor hallway where Picasso was staying, room 19, they stopped to say goodnight.

"Do you want me to walk you to your room," asked Picasso?

Monet smiled and gave his hand a warm squeeze.

"I'll be okay," she said. "Good night and have sweet dreams of your ranch."

He nodded and watched Monet disappear behind the gold door to the stairwell before he went into his own room for the night.

Monet walked up the stairs to the second floor and down the hall until she reached her room, number 28.

She put the key in the door and turned the knob, she pushed it open and walked inside. Monet switched on the lights and saw in the center of the room two queen sized beds. They looked comfortable with a clean, white quilt and matching, fluffy pillows. There was a desk over in the corner of the room and soft overstuffed chair.

Monet walked over on the soft, white carpet to an oak dresser and pulled out the drawers. There was enough space to store one's clothes, but since she was only staying the one night, she didn't have to worry about unpacking.

Monet was happy with the room. It wasn't overdone like the rest of the hotel, but it was very comfortable and clean. In her mind that is all you needed for just staying the night.

After doing her evening routine, Monet found she wasn't tired yet. She looked at the clock and saw it was 11:30. She sat and looked at her surroundings as an idea came into her head.

She crossed the room to where her purse was sitting, opened it and reached inside. She grabbed the key in her hand and ran her fingers over it.

Curiosity got the best of her as she took both of the keys and left her room to go to the West Wing.

When she arrived on the other side of the hotel, Monet walked down the second-floor hallway, that looked identical to the East's. When she reached door number 28, she took out the key with the black and gold tag (which was different than the white and gold one for the East Wing) and put it in the lock. She paused a moment before she turned the key in the lock. She wanted to make sure her mind was in the right place. What if everything she had ever wanted was on the other side of the door? What if the temptation was too great and she gave in? What would the hotel expect in return?

Monet took a few deep breaths and pushed open the door.

She switched on the lights and saw in the center of the room a four-poster bed with deep red curtains cascading from the sides. A gold-leaf dresser, table, and mirror were positioned around the room.

Monet couldn't believe her eyes. The vanity that was situated in the corner of the room was the same one her best friend Marcia Silvers had when she was a little girl. She had always wanted it. She walked over so she could run her hands over the smooth, oval mirror and touch the silver brush and comb set that was sitting on top of the beautiful mahogany vanity. She couldn't help herself as she ran the brush through her curls.

Monet put the brush down and walked to wardrobe that was on the opposite wall. She ran her hands over the intricate carvings that had a beautiful apple tree motif etched in them.

She opened the double doors and was surprised to see clothes hanging inside. She ran her hands over the garments and separated them so she could get a better look. Her heart fluttered as she pulled out a white, silk, wrap dress.

"These look like the exact clothes I had dreamed about when I was a little girl," she said hugging the dress as it reminded her of a dress actress Gretta Garbo would have worn.

She put the garment back and walked over the black and white patterned carpet that led to the bathroom that had a white and gray marble floor and the same extravagant style of furnishings.

Monet turned and looked at herself in the mirror. She was smiling, but the smile quickly faded away.

"This isn't you," she said to her reflection. "Sure, you want this stuff, but it's just stuff."

Monet knew what she had to do. She switched off the light and walked out of the bathroom. She took one more look around at the room before she left and locked the door behind her. Sure, her curiosity had gotten the better of her, but now at least she knew she had made the right decision in the beginning.

After a few hours of blissful sleep Monet sat straight up in bed with a start. She thought maybe what she heard was part of her dream. She held her breath and waited in the darkness to see if it would happen again.

"Crack"

She looked over at the clock and it read 1:15 a.m.

"Crack"

Monet reached for a light, but stopped cold because she heard a faint, but urgent knocking on her door.

She wasn't sure if she should get out of her bed. What if the hotel was falling apart and it would swallow her whole because the foundation was cracking? What if a mass murderer was on the loose? He, or she, could be knocking on her door.

The faint knocking happened again.

Monet gingerly put one foot on the floor and transferred her weight as she squinted her eyes and held her breath. The floor was stable. She could take the hotel falling apart off her list of sources for the cracking noise.

The gentle knocking continued, except this time it seemed more frantic.

She threw her sheets all the way back and deftly tip-toed toward the door.

She stretched and looked out the peephole. The hallway was mostly dark except for a lamp on a nearby table and a few dimly lit wall sconces.

Standing there in the shadows was a teen boy with light brown hair and blond highlights.

"Please let me in," he pleaded through the door.

Monet felt her heart soften. She was always the type of person to take in stray animals. It was part of her DNA, so how could she resist now.

She undid the deadbolt and opened the door slightly.

The teen, who looked like a little boy trying to escape from thunderstorms in the night, pushed past her, slammed the door and forced his back against it as he breathed heavily trying to get as much air into his lungs as possible.

"It really isn't all the bad," Monet said.

She walked over to him and put a reassuring hand on his shoulder as a form of comfort.

The teen slowly turned his head away from the peephole he was looking out of toward Monet so she could look into his eyes, his bottom jaw was still shaking.

"You have no idea," he said.

Monet screwed up her lips in a doubtful smile and gently guided him to sit in the easy chair that was over by the window.

"Let me get you a drink of water. What's your name, anyway?" her voice asked yelling over the running water of the bathroom.

"It's Pollock," he said.

Monet smiled to herself in the mirror. There was no better name for this on edge boy. Pollock's paintings of messy splatters perfectly aligned with the teen's nervous energy.

She extended the water glass toward him.

"Drink it," she said. "It might make you feel better."

He took the glass with a grateful nod and drank it as she made herself comfortable on the chair opposite him and tightened the belt around her robe.

"What has you so afraid," she asked?

Pollock put the glass on the side table and moved his wispy dirty-blond hair away from his eyes.

"It always happens at night. Things change around here then. During the day everything is fine, but at night it is different," he said.

Monet sat and thought for a while, playing with a tassel on a nearby pillow.

"How many nights have you been here?" she asked.

"This is night number two. Last night it wasn't as loud. Now it seems like it is filling the hallways and is in between the walls."

Monet looked at the frightened boy, he reminded her of Charlie, someone she babysat for as a teenager.

"Pollock, where are your parents," she asked?

Pollock looked at her. His expression had changed from one of being frightened to being insulted.

"They aren't here. I'm traveling to VidCon by myself. I am eighteen, after all."

When Monet looked at him, she could tell he was hurt by her question. But the more she thought about it she wasn't sure if it was hurt or something else. Maybe she had insulted his pride for thinking how young he was. But it wasn't her fault, the young completion and shaggy haircut made him seem younger than a person right on the verge of adulthood. Maybe he was lying about his age, but she wasn't going to question him.

"Right," she said trying to clear the air a little.

Monet rose to her full height and walked to Pollock. She gently reached out for his hand and lead him to the door.

"We are going to settle this so we can both get some sleep," she said.

Pollock ripped his hand from hers before she could move him too close to the door.

"You are a crazy lady if you think I'm going back out there right now," he said leaning against the dresser with his arms folded across his chest.

"It's just a noise," she said trying to calm his nerves. "It's just like thunder. How can a noise hurt you?"

Pollock turned his head and huffed with disgust. "You haven't seen what I saw. You have no idea what that 'sound' can do."

Monet looked at him for a moment before responding, "Fine. I'll go on my own then. You can stay here and crawl under the bed to get away from The Bogeyman."

As Monet turned to walk toward the door, she could hear a huff followed by a groan.

"Fine. I don't want you going by yourself. An older woman could get hurt, out there," said Pollock.

Monet let the 'older woman' comment glide off her back as she smiled to herself knowing the insult had hit its target.

Monet opened the door slowly and looked to the left and saw nothing but more individual room doors along the corridor and the large gold door at the end that no doubt led to a stairwell, the same as the one she came through on the other end of the hallway.

"We are going to talk to our friend Raphael. He should have some answers," she said.

Monet and Pollock walked down the hall. Immediately for some reason, she could feel the hairs on the back of her neck start to stand up. She shrugged it off as the teen was just making her nerves stand on edge.

He was such a loose cannon. Monet wasn't sure which way his moods were going to swing, and she hated being caught off guard. But, despite his teenage emotions, she had a soft spot for him.

The duo made a left and walked toward the door at the end of the hallway so they could go down the flight of stairs into the lobby.

Monet wrapped her hand around the cold metal of the knob, turned it and gave a push. It wouldn't budge. She tried again, but the door refused to give.

"I told you. Nothing good happens here at night, said Pollock who had pushed Monet's hand off the knob and tried it himself. Monet couldn't help but smirk when he couldn't open it either.

"Let's try the other one," she said bound and determined to get to the root of what was going on.

She looked at Pollock. She could see he was starting to trust her more.

"I'm not some crazy old lady, you know," she said.

"I know," he said. "I trust you."

She nodded and went down the other end of the hallway.

When they reached the end of the corridor, Pollock tried the door, and it yielded the same results.

They both sighed and seemed discouraged.

"Well, I guess that's why God gave us elevators," she said.

They both walked to the middle of the hallway.

Monet pushed the elevator button. Just like it had been waiting for them, the doors slid open with a happy ding.

The two walked inside as the gold gates slammed shut and descended on its own taking the two guests to an unknown destination.

Munch used to love swimming until that one summer. Now, she was trying to get comfortable in the water again.

The way her ears plugged with water, jamming the sounds of the world from entering her thoughts, and the weightlessness made her feel protected.

As she floated, her hair skimmed the water like a bottle of ink spilled in the ocean.

She looked around the room at the alabaster statues who stood sentry around the pool and gazed through the glass ceiling. She saw the darkness stretched above with stars looking like pinholes letting in light.

A door opened across the room from where she was bobbing in the center of the pool.

She craned her neck to look behind her to see who had walked in.

"Hey, Kahlo," she said.

Kahlo waved to her as she started to take off her robe to unveil a bright red, one-piece bathing suit underneath.

"Couldn't sleep either, Munch," she asked?

"Nope. And even this doesn't seem to help," she said.

Kahlo stepped into the calming water and glided over to the girl spinning in the center.

"Tomorrow's the big day, huh?" asked Munch as she lazily floated on the water.

"Yep. Tomorrow morning, I head out for Hollywood."

Munch positioned herself better so she could see Kahlo.

"Nervous at all?"

"Why would I be. I have all that I need, plus I was born to be an actress."

The two of them floated in silence for a while, letting the water flow over them.

"To tell you the truth, I am a little nervous. I mean, I have to think I'm going to make it, because if not then why bother at all."

"True," replied Munch.

Silence again as the two women, one more of a teenager than the other, continued to float in the pool.

"I think I'm switching," said Munch.

Now it was Kahlo's turn to be surprised.

"Why? I thought you were happy in your room, plus I thought you were going to leave tomorrow for your internship in New York City."

Munch let Kahlo's words wash over her and made her doubt her plan. She moved her arms, so she floated in a circle for a while; giving her more time to think before she responded.

"I don't like how I feel in the room," she said. "It doesn't make sense. There is everything that I could possibly want, or that I have ever wanted in the whole world. But I don't know, it seems like things are different now. The summer I lost my brother, I thought life would be easier if I had all the money, clothes, and stuff I wanted. But, being here and actually having it has given me a sort of anxiety. I don't want to feel like that anymore.

"Maybe, just maybe, I can escape this feeling if I move out of the prison of stuff and into a room on the other wing. A fresh start. Just like the internship. So, I think I want to take a few days to stay here and get my head on straight."

Kahlo was surprised at her change in heart.

She looked at the younger girl in the pool with her and was surprised at how someone could be so naive and idealistic. When you have everything, you want, you don't look a gift horse in the mouth.

"Yeah, well not me, baby girl. The next time you see me will be on the big screen," said Kahlo.

The two floated again in silence. Like two ships trying to find their mooring in the calm sea.

They started to float away from each other.

"I just feel like I have to trust my gut," said Munch.

There was no response.

"Kahlo, you there," she asked?

Silence hung in the air. Even the vacant looking statues seemed to hold their breath waiting for a response.

Munch lifted her head from the water and up righted herself to tread water.

"Kahlo, where did you go," she asked?

She looked all over the room and couldn't find her friend that was only a few feet away from her moments ago. Her robe was still draped over the silver lounger where she had left it when she walked in.

Panic rose in Munch's chest. She tried to still her mind, but all of her emotions fought against her. Images of being underwater, trying to pull someone to the surface, bubbles coming up from under the water, and a woman crying came at her like a freight train.

She could tell a full-blown panic attack was coming so she swam to the side of the pool to hang onto until it passed.

*Breathe in four. Hold for four. Breathe out eight.*

No matter how many breaths she took, Munch couldn't change the fact a woman had just disappeared into thin air right before her eyes, and this was the second time she had lost someone to the water.

The doors to the elevator slid open to reveal another hallway.

"I didn't press anything," said Pollock.

He looked over at Monet who was equally confused.

She poked her head outside of the elevator and took in the surroundings.

The hall looked very similar to the second floor where her room was, but something felt off. The red carpet seemed darker, and the gold trim was tarnished.

She turned back toward Pollock.

"I've been to the West Wing before and it didn't look like this," she said.

He shook his head.

"Elevators don't move sideways," he said.

Monet nodded in agreement.

She stepped through the double doors with Pollock behind her. They heard a ding as the elevator doors shut sealing their fate.

Monet turned around in a panic and hit the button to try and get the doors to open again, but it was useless. The elevator car had left and now they were stranded on an unknown floor.

Pollock shivered.

"I don't like this one bit. I reminds me of a time I went with a friend... well, at least someone who I thought was my friend, and we explored an old factory. It had the same creep factor."

Pollock continued to stand there. Like he was processing something in his head, but he had a hard time trying to figure it out. Like a fog was rolling in when he looked back at that memory.

"We could try and take the stairs on this floor," said Monet shaking Pollock from his thoughts.

He nodded and followed her down the hall.

That's when they heard it again.

"CRACK"

This time it seemed louder. The air had a strange electricity around them, and there was a smell like something just starting to singe.

The duo stopped dead in their tracks.

"CRACK"

It seemed closer as they remained the only ones in the hallway.

"What should we do," asked Monet?

Pollock looked up and down the hallway.

"CRACK"

The time between each noise was growing shorter. Whatever it was would make its way to them any minute.

He turned around and tried the doorknob behind him. His hands were so sweaty he was having a hard time getting a grip on the brass knob.

"CRACK"

"Turn faster," said Monet in a rushed but hushed voice.

After several attempts, Pollock wrapped his fingers and his palm around the nob and pushed hard as it gave way and they both scurried inside before shutting and locking the barrier behind them.

Pollock and Monet stood in the darkness for a while catching their breath. They looked at each other and started to smile and laugh a little. No doubt it was the adrenaline subsiding that brought on this little amount of joy.

"I'll keep a watch out of a small crack in the door while you try and find a light to see where we are," said Monet.

Pollock nodded as Monet turned her back to open the door a slight crack and peer out the opening.

"We might be safe now, but I want to be sure," she said. Her voice was muffled against the cold wood of the door.

Pollock let his eyes adjust to the darkness for a moment.

"Are you an East Winger, too?" asked Monet trying to distract them from being afraid.

"No. Well, I started out as one, but then I changed my mind," he said, his voice bouncing all over the room as he continued his quest. "The day after I checked in, I had to see what was going on with the other side of the building, it was too tempting to pass up. Once I saw it, I knew I had to switch."

Monet was silent for a moment as she continued to monitor what was going on in the hall.

"In the room was everything I could have possibly wanted, high-tech video equipment, a sweet computer setup, and even VIP tickets to VIDCON. So, I went right down and told Raphael that I wanted to switch, and never looked back. But that is how I make a lot of decisions in life. I trust my gut and just don't look back."

Monet mumbled an acknowledgment what he just said.

"Did you check out your West room," he asked Monet.

With her face still pressed toward the door she said, "I did. It had all the things I wanted since I was a little girl. Things I envied for years."

"You switching?"

"I thought about it a lot. I almost did, but when I looked at it, those things were just chains for me. They made me envious for so many years when I was younger, that I didn't get to enjoy the things I had. I don't need that in my life now."

Pollock continued to search in the darkness and grope over the furniture. So far, he found an overstuffed chair, a coat rack, and what he thought was a television, but no lights.

With a thump, Pollock bumped his knee into what he determined to be a dresser. His hands glided over the slick surface until he came to something with a square base. He caressed his hand all the way to where he found a switch. He pushed it with a click, and nothing happened.

Pollock let out a sigh.

"Typical of this stupid place," he said. "It reminds me of this amusement park I used to work for in the summers. There were problems getting things to work right sometimes and we had to go underneath the rides and it would be so dark we would bump into things."

An idea flashed into Pollock head. He gave up his search and went over to Monet.

"Let me out of the room for a minute," he said trying to inch himself between her and the door so he could leave.

Monet turned away from the hallway and looked at him.

"Are you crazy? You have no idea what is out there. We are trying to keep ourselves safe and you want to go into the hallway and possibly run into God-knows-what?"

Pollock looked at her, and in the little light that was creeping through the crack in the door Monet could see something that she didn't like.

"I want to get my camera. This is a goldmine of content for my channel. Just wait here. I will be quick and whoever, or whatever is making that sound won't find me."

With that he pushed Monet aside and squeezed out the door. He paused for a moment before he turned left and headed toward the gold door that led to the stairwell.

He had only gone past two doors when the lights started to flicker with an electric hum. The already dark corridor was enveloped in even more darkness than before.

Pollock stopped in his tracks as a flicker of doubt flowed over him.

He started walking again, until he saw a dark figure blocking his path to the door.

Monet saw him start and saw the figure, too. She held her breath for a moment before she yelled to him.

"Come back now, Pollock. It isn't safe!"

The boy dismissed her with a wave of his hand. He was hell-bent on getting his camera. Opportunities like this don't often exist.

He approached the figure slowly as it too began to inch toward Pollock. The darkness around the figure seemed to part around him for an even darker figure to cut through. The air around was bursting with the feeling of electricity and as the figure got closer it smelled like burning plastic and mechanical grease.

Suddenly, recognition flashed over Pollock's face.

His mouth became dry and as he tried to produce a sound from his throat, the only thing that would come out was a croak that said, "Adam?"

Monet, still in the room with the door open a little wider now yelled out for Pollock again, but this time her words in the air seemed suspended in aspic.

The lights went out completely and the hallway was plunged into darkness for a moment before all the lights came surging back to life. In that brief moment, when Monet lost sight of Pollock, he disappeared. He was nowhere to be found.

"CRACK"

She called out again to the empty hallway.

"Pollock."

There was no answer.

She left her post at the door and ventured a little into the hallway, but he was nowhere to be found.

Her blood started to pump so fast and furious she could hear it rushing in her ears. Her body was telling her to get out of that hallway as fast as she could; something wasn't right.

"CRACK"

Monet had to make a choice. She had to either stay where she was or try and escape and possibly face the source of the noise.

Having made her decision, she gingerly walked to the end of the hallway.

Monet started walking toward destination when she had to hold her breath to keep herself from crying out. There was another figure blocking her escape. She squinted and realized it was Raphael, or so she thought. It looked like him, but he appeared so different.

His hair was the same, but he had a type of black makeup in the shape of a bar over his eyes. He wore what she would call a red and black corset with black leather straps hanging from the bottom over top of a black billowing skirt that went all the way to the floor.

She saw him raise his hand in the air and then bring it down hard and quickly.

"CRACK!"

Monet jumped. She wasn't sure how he was making the noise, but she knew he was responsible for it.

"CRACK!"

This time, she paid closer attention and saw he had a whip in the hand he was plummeting toward the ground.

As he glided closer, Monet could see his eyes were dead; there was no life behind them.

Before he could close the gap even more between the two of them, Monet turned and ran toward the other gold door at the end of the hallway.

Just like it had happened with Pollock, her hands, wet with sweat, had a hard time gripping the knob and turning.

Monet started to panic even more as she could feel Raphael getting closer and closer to her.

Finally, she was able to get a tight grip on the knob and pushed it open before escaping to the stairwell and slamming it shut behind her putting her full bodyweight against her to make sure it would stay closed.

Monet knew she had to find someone else to talk to about this. After all, she felt there was safety in numbers and together they would be able to leave. She wanted to get her things and car keys so she could leave this hell hotel and never look back.

She left the gold door and navigated her way to the first floor of the East Wing.

When Monet reached the door frame of the room, she was surprised to see it was wide open. Standing in the middle of the room, tucking in the corners of a crisp, white sheet was a maid. She didn't seem bothered that people were disappearing or there was a crazy man with a whip walking up and down the halls.

Monet looked puzzled and checked the room number. She wanted to make sure she was in the right place, and it turned out she was.

"Excuse me," Monet croaked out, her throat dry and her breath heavy.

The maid looked up from her task seeing Monet entering the room. Monet saw it was similar to hers but had a few differences. Clothes were strewn about and empty bottles and food containers were thrown on the floor haphazardly. Monet felt bad for the woman who was going to have to clean up this mess.

"Do you know where I can find the gentleman that is staying in this room," she asked?

The maid looked at her and smiled. "He is no longer here," she said.

Monet wrinkled her brow and looked puzzled.

"Where would he go in the middle of the night," she asked?

"He is no longer here," the maid repeated. A smile similar to Raphael's drew across her face.

If it wasn't for her fluid movements and breathing pattern, Monet would have sworn she was talking to an animatronic.

As if sensing her puzzlement, the maid added, "He won't be back. He moved on."

Monet surveyed Picasso's room. His suitcase was still there with a lot of his things.

"Why didn't he take his belongings," she asked the housekeeper?

The woman stopped what she was doing, looked at Monet and with the same, grotesque smile said, "He won't need them where he is going."

Monet looked at the woman in surprise. Here she was doing something that would be considered normal, a housekeeper cleaning a room in a hotel. But, when you put it in context that it was the middle of the night and a person just disappeared into thin air, then it seemed repulsive. It was like taking ordinary, every-day-life and perverting it. But that wasn't the worst part. The fact this housekeeper really didn't care, made Monet fume. She was going to get to the bottom of this. The only person who would have the answers is the same person she tried to avoid only moments ago.

The maid had decided she gave an efficient amount of an answer and returned to her cleaning duties.

Monet looked back at the woman and decided it was better to deal with this through Raphael, no matter how terrifying that might be.

Munch was able to settle her breathing. She loosened the grip she had on the side of the pool that was causing her knuckles to turn white. The muscles in her arms were starting to cramp and they were happy when she granted them relief and started to tread water in the deep end of the pool.

She looked around the area trying to find an answer about what should she do about Kahlo's disappearance.

Munch swam to the shallow end and climbed out of the pool dripping wet, trying not to slip on the marble floor as she went to get her towel and cover up.

*Who in their right mind puts a marble floor around a pool?*

When she reached her towel, she roughly ran it through her long, dark, curly hair and then down the rest of her body before wrapping herself in the robe she took from her room.

As she was tying a knot with the belt around her curvy frame, she looked toward the lobby and saw a woman marching toward the front desk. From what she could tell, this woman had a bone to pick with someone and everybody else should move out of the way.

*She's pissed about something.*

Not wanting to be alone anymore, Munch slipped on her sandals and walked to the door of the pool, making flip-flop noises echoing off the cavernous room that seemed like a crypt to her now.

"Ding. Ding."

The noise was filling the lobby as the angry woman rang the bell, not taking a break for anyone to appear behind the desk before she rang it again.

Munch crept closer trying to stay out of the woman's line of sight.

"Raphael," the woman yelled!

In between the dinging and yelling, the tall man appeared behind the desk in his usual red velvet coat and a black button-down shirt. Munch couldn't help but wonder if he ever slept since he was here in the daytime and at this early hour in the morning.

His hair was quaffed as usual and the same pleasant smile was on his face as he placed his hand over the bell, before Monet could ring it again.

"Mrs. Monet. A pleasure to see you again. What can I help you with?"

Monet huffed with a smirk as if she couldn't believe he would have the audacity to say such a thing to her.

"Oh yes. It's been so long since you last saw me, right Raphael? I'm surprised you could get down here so quickly and change your clothes so fast."

Monet's voice spat out the words like venom. She was a woman who had enough of whatever crazy place this was. All the while, Raphael, never changed his expression. He was the picture of congeniality and serenity.

Munch watched from a distance as he remained composed and calm, a true professional, as he tried to diffuse the angry guest.

"What is it I can do to make your stay more pleasant," he asked? "Are you unhappy with your room? Do you want to change to the other wing?"

Monet leaned her left hand on the desk and put her other on her hip.

"I want to know why people keep on disappearing on me. First, I lost Pollock right in the middle of the hallway. He just 'poofed' right into thin-air, and then when I went to find Picasso, the maid said he had moved on, but all of his things are still there. I want to know what the hell is going on."

Munch's ears perked up at hearing this woman talk about people disappearing.

*Just like Kahlo.*

She inched closer to the desk, trying to not make it obvious that she was listening to their conversation.

"Oh, is that all?" he asked treating Monet like she had just made a simple request like more towels or a morning wake up call.

His flippant tone and widening smile were starting to grate on Monet's nerves.

"They made their final decision on their rooms," he said. "Is there anything else I can do for you?"

Munch was now standing next to Monet at the desk, both of them staring at Raphael puzzled.

"What does that mean?" Munch asked, joining in the conversation for the first time. "They made their final room decisions?"

Raphael now narrowed his gaze to Munch, which made him look even more like a bird bearing down on its prey. Munch could tell he didn't like being challenged, but was professional enough to tamp that emotion deep, down inside.

However, he couldn't prevent the sickly, widening grin from spreading across his face again. It was the type of grin that sent shivers down Munch's spine. She couldn't' put her finger on it, but something made her feel uneasy.

"Ladies, I'm sorry for the confusion and the discomfort this has caused. Please head over to the bar and have a cocktail on me. That should calm your nerves," he said.

Raphael extended his hand toward the bar on the other side of the room.

"A Pinot Noir for you Mrs. Monet, and a virgin Pina Colada for you, Ms. Munch, correct?" They both nodded surprised at how he remembered their preferred orders. They were even more surprised when they arrived at the bar to see the two drinks sitting there waiting for them.

Not knowing what else to do and thinking cooler heads might prevail they took their seats at the stools and silently sipped their beverages trying to comprehend what had happened.

Munch broke the silence first.

"Just so you know, you aren't crazy," she said turning to Monet who was swirling the wine around in her glass.

Monet put down her drink, looked toward the younger woman and raised an eyebrow in mock insult.

"Not saying you thought you were crazy, but I just didn't want you to feel like you were alone," she responded before taking a sip of her cold drink.

Monet responded by taking a long gulp of wine. The warm tannins ran down her throat where it warmed her belly.

"I just don't understand how a person can be right in front of you one minute and gone the next," she said.

Munch nodded in agreement.

"Same happened to me. I was in a pool with someone, I turned around and she was gone."

Munch wiped the sweat off the outside of the tumbler, as Monet swirled the burgundy liquid around her glass leaving a stain along its trail.

A smile came across Monet's face as she thought of something.

"I like your art," she said.

Munch looked over at the woman. She didn't understand what she meant at first, but then realization dawned on her. She returned the smile.

"Yeah, 'The Scream.' It's pretty ironic," she said returning her attention back to her beverage.

Monet looked at her quizzically.

"I deal with a lot of anxiety, so I feel like I am always internally screaming about something," she said.

Monet sadly nodded. The girl sitting in front of her may have only been a teenager, but it seemed like she had lived many lifetimes.

"I have always loved Monet. My parents would take me to a botanical garden when I was younger and my favorite part was the water lilies," she said. "I guess I had forgotten about that until now."

The two women sat in silence. Raphael was now gone to do whatever it was he did at 4:30 in the morning, leaving the only awake souls to their own devices at the bar.

"It's funny how life works out. It took me until this very moment to feel content about things," said Monet.

"How so?"

"I spent a lot of my life trying to prove something to people. To try to always be better and show that I was doing the best I could. I was always proving myself to others. But I just realized that I was envying other people and their confidence. I was so focused outward, that I never really thought, 'What if all I need is what I have right now?'" she said.

Monet smiled and thought of something that she kept to herself.

"I guess the question that Raphael had asked me about wanting to switch rooms, made me realize this. The grass isn't always greener, and true happiness can be found if you take the time to live in the present," she said. "It's just like these rooms. I've decided I'm not going to switch because I like what I have. I don't always need to have this desire for something different. And that doesn't make me seem less driven."

Munch looked down at her glass. The liquid was starting to dry up and she was left with a lot more ice than anything else.

"I wish I was as fearless as you, Monet," she said.

Munch turned to look at her drinking companion and was surprised to see she wasn't there. Her empty wine glass was the only evidence she was ever sitting next to her.

She looked behind the bar and underneath of it but couldn't find Monet. She called out her name and spun around in her seat to look at the lobby.

No one was around.

*She couldn't have left that fast. Not again.*

Munch could feel her breathing start to constrict as it had before. She hated being left alone.

*This can't be happening.*

*Four counts in. Hold for four. Eight counts out.*

Munch stood up from her stool on wobbly legs.

She leaned on the back of the seat and tried to steady herself.

She concentrated as she put one foot in front of the other and walked toward the front desk.

*People just don't disappear. This can't be happening.*

The room began to swirl in her vision and a haze on her periphery began to form. She steadied herself on end tables and the backs of the high velvet chairs until she reached the front desk. She needed help, and she needed it now.

Munch thought about ringing the bell, just like Monet had done earlier, but didn't want to waste time for Raphael to walk out.

She weaved her way over to the side of the desk and then went behind it.

Munch had just pulled back the curtain that covered the entrance to one of the rooms behind the front desk when she saw a man seated on a white chair drinking from a teacup in a room surrounded by books,

He seemed familiar as much as she could recognize through the blurriness that was in her eyes. Even her concentration was starting to go as the familiar sound of blood rushing in her ears began to pulse.

That's when she remembered.

"Simon," she said before hitting the ground and the world going very dark.

Munch opened her eyes to see she was reclined on a camel-colored lounger in what appeared to be a library.

White bookshelves were carved into the walls and a few table lamps were scattered over the open area.

Sitting across from her, in a matching wingback chair was the man she had only met once before, but he seemed so familiar to her. Like they had known each other for a long time.

"How are you feeling?" he asked getting up from his chair and walking over to her.

Munch started to sit up, but felt her head begin to swim again.

The man put his arm behind her back to steady her.

"Maybe you should lay down rest a little longer," he said.

The man helped lay her back down, returned to his seat, and resumed his drinking from his teacup while keeping a watchful eye on Munch.

With her vision beginning to return, Munch saw he was wearing a seersucker suit with a light blue pocket square peeking out of the pocket. A rather cheerful ensemble that didn't seem to fit the rest of Hotel Arcadia.

"Where am I," she asked?

"Doesn't this place look familiar to you," he replied?

Munch couldn't tell, but it was like he was enjoying the fact she was kind of out of it.

She looked around the area from her reclined position. The books, the lamps, and even the artwork by Picasso, Monet, Kahlo, Munch, and Pollock seemed familiar but she couldn't recall it.

"You've been here before," he said. "Try and remember."

Munch screwed her eyes tight as she fought with her memory. Visions of being in this room talking about water and second chances swam in and out of her mind like circling sharks.

"It's starting to come back, isn't it?" he said leaning forward and placing his cup on the coffee table between them.

Suddenly, something clicked together in Munch's head and she bolted upright to a sitting position.

"Simon," she said.

He smiled. A warm, friendly smile that was so different than the one Raphael always offered.

"Welcome home, Liz."

Time had passed and Liz was starting to feel a little more like herself, well as best as she could having just gained back her memory. Simon had gotten her a cup of tea and a cinnamon roll to eat while they talked.

"I tried to warn you that day at Lakewood. I didn't feel like you were ready yet. But, in the end, you didn't listen. You just had to come back anyway," he said.

Liz took another drink of lavender tea, the hot liquid warmed not just her body, but her soul, too.

"The others, are they like me," she asked?

Simon took a long sip of his tea before he placed it on the saucer he was holding in his right hand.

"No. They were just lost souls that ended up becoming pawns in the game," he said.

When Liz stared at him blankly, Simon sighed because he was just realizing she remembered less than he thought.

"Adam and I, at the behest of our masters, were charged to persuade people to be on our respective 'sides.' Because humans are born with free will, we had to choose people we felt would choose our sides in the long run," he said.

Simon took a break to take a sip of tea before continuing.

"The Designer started to feel like Adam and The Dark Architect were cheating and trying to tip the scales in their favor," he said. "When Marjorie, Emma, Danny, and Jonas showed up, we knew Adam had been working overtime.

"That is why we eventually let them choose their fate instead of being assigned their final destination," he said.

Liz looked down at the tea. Things were starting to sound familiar. Like she had heard this before.

Simon continued, "The East Wing represented the side of The Designer. It was pure and comfortable. The pool represented the life-giving waters He offers.

"The West Wing was the side of The Dark Architect. The rooms were filled to the brim with the desires and greatest dreams of the guests. The apple from the tree of knowledge, if you will. Only when people renounced these temptations did they get to move on to a better place. This was their final test. However, if the person gave in, like Jonas and Emma, they were sent to become slaves to their possessions and their new master."

Simon's face filled with sadness as he thought of those tortured souls.

"Marjorie and Danny made their right choices. So now they will get to experience their greatest dreams," he added.

Liz balanced the cup on her knee.

"So, Marjorie will get to go to Las Vegas and Danny will get his cattle ranch," she asked?

Simon nodded, "In a sense, yes. Well, at least that is what their experiences will be like."

Liz was happy to hear this. She knew Marjorie only a little but was happy to find out they were going to live their dreams.

"When we saw you walk into the hotel, I have to admit I was a little worried. It seemed like Adam was up to his tricks again trying to persuade people to his side. But, after seeing you renounce various temptations we had hope again. We felt you might be the one to restore the balance."

"Liz's head snapped up and she looked at Simon.

"What makes me different than the others," she asked?

Simon smiled again and it brought comfort to Liz.

"This is the second time you have been here. Each time, it has been your choice," he said. "The first time you were soaking wet with water in your lungs after you tried to rescue your little brother from the bottom of the pool. The Designer sent you back to your mother who couldn't bear to lose both of her children. He showed your family great mercy.

"But, before you went back, we had a similar conversation in this same room where you were charged with trying to find out why the darkness has such a tight grip in Seraphim Falls."

Liz stayed silent for a moment.

"I never did that," she said.

Liz felt awful finding out she had broken one of her promises; especially about something that seemed so important. But she was just a teenager, how was she supposed to find out about the darkness in her hometown?

"I feel like you are going to offer me a deal," she said.

Simon slowly nodded. His side wasn't used to making deals.

"He is losing, Liz. We aren't sure what this means long term, but it could be bad," he said talking about his boss.

"What do I have to do," she asked?

"The choice is yours. You can go back to Seraphim Falls and fix things and tip the scale in our favor," he said.

"Or…"

Simon looked at Liz as he leaned forward and peered into her eyes.

"Or you could stay here and face your ultimate fate."

Liz swirled the remainder of her tea. It swished around the cup like a tempest threatening to bubble out of control.

She looked up from her tea across at Simon just as she heard a loud "CRACK" in the distance.

CPSIA information can be obtained
at www.ICGtesting.com
Printed in the USA
BVHW042105060521
606681BV00008B/100